WE: SMOKE

Michael Fawcett

MICHAEL FAWCETT

outskirts
press

Outskirts Press, Inc.
http://www.outskirtspress.com

ISBN: 978-1-4787-1539-9

Cover Image by Michael Fawcett

Outskirts Press and the "OP" logo are trademarks belonging to Outskirts Press, Inc.

PRINTED IN THE UNITED STATES OF AMERICA

CHAPTER 1

G oing out to breakfast was always a pleasure. Sure beat cooking eggs with bacon at home. Had to take everything out, put it all away again. Hope you didn't burn everything in the process. Had to clean everything up when you got finished. Wife would be all over you if you didn't! Going out to a diner was much preferred. They did all the cooking for you. Never had a bad meal when I went out! Paleyville, down the road a piece, had my favorite diner.

"Well, how did you do?" Paul walked into the diner, sat down across from me in the booth. His usual cob pipe was in the corner of his mouth, with a small whiff of smoke curling out.

"It was a good night for me. I didn't lose a cent," I replied. It was Monday morning, around seven thirty, and the regulars were just starting to drift in. Another miserable day, still raining with fog. Friday night through Sunday late had been all goop. It rained, snowed, hailed, sleeted, more rain, plus a ton of thick soup fog you couldn't see ten feet through. Just real goop weather days.

Joe-Bob Rice turned on his counter stool, half a mouth full of blueberry pancakes, trying to wash it all down with orange juice before he talked.

"Whazzah hell are you talking about, *Road Cone*, you guys didn't even play!" He was right. We didn't play at all.

The temperature couldn't make up its mind between 27 and 34 degrees. The weather was total crap yesterday. On Sunday afternoon we decided to flip a coin on what we should do. It took four tosses out of seven—a hard decision: we would stay home, in the warmth, with a blanket over our heads! We didn't cancel. Cribbage playing is never canceled. It was postponed until the next Sunday!

The game of cribbage is a mainstay diet in Vermont. Sort of like putting cream in your coffee. Everyone did it, or played the game. It was in your blood! Had to have it at least once a week to stay in good health.

Sunday nights, our dastardly group of misfits would always gather to play cribbage. We would start at 7 in the evening, ending as close to 10 P.M. as the games would allow. We all met at the firehouse. We played a dollar a game. It was singles or partners, depending on how many buzzards gathered on the fence. There were usually seven or eight of us.

We played all down-to-business games, and

played them fast. No one was safe. There was always someone ready to pounce on any seemingly innocent card played, gain two extra points, forge ahead by one. If you or your twosome lost, losers pay a buck to the left. If you won, collect from the right.

When playing with partners, cards were dealt out to see who sat where, with an ugly bloke as a partner. When my card came up, many tears were shed. Most were tears of happiness—they didn't get me. One old buzzard's tears would be those of pain, suffering, and sadness.

"Tough luck, sucker! You get *Road Cone*!" It was supposed to be a fun evening out with friends!

My luck at cribbage for the last month—actually three months—had been so horrific they all smiled when they saw me coming. That, or they went and hid someplace. I've put at least two of their kids through a year's worth of college! Sometimes just a dollar, sometimes two on a skunk. On a good night I'd only fork out seven or eight bucks. On a bad night, well ... a few dollars more. The cribbage gods have not been kind to me at all. It's been a long, dark, lonely ... expensive road! They all smile at the end of a game.

"Pleasure doing business with Yah!"

"Hey, we don't play, I break even. That makes it a good night for me! Right?" I replied.

I ordered my usual breakfast—very burnt hash, two eggs over, an English muffin, OJ, coffee; oh, and don't forget the side order of bacon "*to go*" for Salty!

Salty was my three-year-old yellow Lab. He went everywhere with me. He gets two pieces of bacon every time we go for breakfast. If he doesn't see bacon when I step outside, his paws go up, doors are locked from the inside—he doesn't let me drive home!

Paul ordered his usual pancakes with real Vermont maple—not that corn syrup crap!—crisp bacon, and coffee. Molly served the breakfast. All was consumed without incident, uneventfully.

I helped Betty, sitting at the counter, cigarette in one hand, pencil in the other, thumping the counter with the eraser end. She was there every morning with her long colorful baggy sweater, scarf, glasses down on nose, working on a couple of her crossword questions. She worked the local crossword in the morning paper. It was her morning ritual to be there on that stool.

She would ask me some weird question about Peru or something. Of course I'd know absolutely nothing about it. Then she would answer it before I had a chance to think, or ask her what the hell she asked me about. I guess I should be thankful. She had a long history with crosswords, and she was good. I had a long history of

"Whazzah Matt-ah U!"—routinely not knowing a thing about whatever it was she just said.

Paul, across from me, was different. He and Betty sort of played a game with each other to see who could come up with the answer first. It had to fit the space, and work with the other letters. Paul would just say the answer without even looking up from his pancakes. Betty would shrug her shoulders, give him a stare, sneak in a smile every so often, and move on to the next word going down. Nothing else said—it was all gain. When she and Paul were on a roll, you just went with it. Crossword was done quickly when those two bit into it.

"Water mammal from Australia—eight letters."

"Platypus."

"Yup! Fits with the 'Y' .... Four letters across, makes a loud noise ..." It would continue until the last square in the far corner ended the ritual for that day. I had my last glug of coffee, paid up, grabbed my bacon in the tinfoil for Salty. I aimed for the outside door. I'd just stepped out into the cold, miserable bleakness, down the three snowy steps to the slush on the sidewalk, when my pocket lit up. Oh goody, something for us! My ears perked right up.

"*Beep, Beep, Beep, Beep* ...... The tone is for Westland ....."

My monitor was squawking at me. I didn't

wait to hear the rest. I'd figure it out when I got to the station. I opened the car door, pushed Salty to the passenger side, red lights turned on, fastened my seat belt, headed north. It was seven miles to the station. I knew I wouldn't be the first one there. Salty was wondering what happened to his bacon.

"Later, Salt. You'll get it later," I said. He first looked disappointed. Then he thought it was a game. I'd hidden his treat somewhere in the car for him. He checked all around his seat. He finally discovered the tinfoil up on the dash on my side. It was out of his reach. He would have to wait patiently.

It was a rescue call. A woman had fallen outside, unknown injuries. The monitor had spoken. Blue Angel Ambulance, our local service, was also toned to respond. Bad ice year, this year. A lot of people going *zip boom*, hurting themselves. Mostly bumps and bruises, but a few people broke bones or something more serious in the process of slip-sliding away.

I got to the station just as our Utility-1 pulled out—lights blazing—responding with four aboard. Our Rescue-1 was already long out of sight. It would be just about on the scene.

Greg was already at the dispatch desk, scribbling notes and answering the squawk from different channels. I had parked, opened the window slightly for Salt, spread the tinfoil for his bacon on his passenger seat. He was happily munching away as I dashed into dispatch.

"*Road Cone*, grab that phone call!"

I grabbed the phone. Greg, at the same time, told Kayle Dispatch that U-1 had responded. R-1 was now on the scene. C-3 was assuming command. Kayle Central Dispatch, the high command of all dispatch operations, acknowledged what Greg said. Greg wrote it all down.

"Yes, OK, yup. No problem." I hung up.

I told Greg it had been Ralph on the line. Ralph was "going direct" to the scene. Ralph always called to say he was going direct. A first-year volunteer that had been told time, and time again, not to go direct. You go to the station first, not direct!

Ralph, being young and ambitious, always wanted to be part of the action. By calling in when our tone went off, he thought he could skip a step, be ahead of the game. He loved going directly to a scene. Wrong Move! Unless you were an officer, all fire and rescue volunteers report to the station first. No exceptions!

A chief would bark at him every time he pulled the stunt of calling in to go direct. Not the correct way we did things around here! Sometimes a chief had to bite and chew four or five times before a "newbie" got it down right. The hammer has come down hard a few times when "Direct Goers" would cause a bottleneck—a scene where unnecessary vehicles would cause a traffic jam, holding necessary emergency vehicles up. Too many vehicles at a scene never helped the situation.

Greg put his name down on the run report with an asterisk next to it, then grabbed for another colored 4x4, scribbled a few new notes, added it to a pile already started. He didn't want to forget anything.

He continued filling in lines, circles, squares on the main run sheet from the small pile of colored paper notes, now spilling onto the floor. It stayed quiet for the next ten minutes. Greg continued writing from his notes, tossing finished ones into the circular file. He wasn't a good basketball player. Many hit the rim and were scattered on the floor.

C-3, our assistant chief, third in command but always first, came on the air, loud with static.

"We are under control, patient's being transported, command is terminated, all units returning in service."

Greg repeated what C-3 had said back to him. Greg then keyed the Central Kayle Dispatch microphone to his right on the dispatch desk. He repeated the same message again to them.

"KAY 445, this is WEL 846."

They returned a "WEL 846."

"All units returning, command terminated." They repeated it back, gave us the correct time.

Greg wrote the time down on the appropriate lines on the run sheet.

We could hear the first truck coming back. It had crossed over Route 45, now was coming down Fireman's Trail. Three hundred yards down was the station on the right. A fairly new building with four large bright red, automatic, push-button bay doors. Greg pressed the correct buttons, door four, followed by door three, slowly rose. George Kratcher, fireman, RIT team interior guy, always hungry, guided both trucks back, lined them up inside their respective bays. George was the only guy in the department that could down two dozen doughnuts in five minutes, then ask if there was anything to eat! Food of any kind was not safe near George!

Bay doors came down. Truck reports were filled out, Patient Care reports turned in, all paperwork properly filed into the appropriate boxes for our department secretary to deal with at a later time. The secretary boxes never got over six or seven calls deep before all the paperwork mysteriously disappeared into the secretary's secret sanctum. All paperwork would be available forever, but never seen again.

It was now quiet on the Eastern Front. Most everyone took off in directions unknown. Greg, George, and I agreed to come back to the station in late afternoon to practice a few games of cribbage. When that time came, all our vehicles parked in the mud, we trudged inside. I went into the dispatch office to grab the three-person cribbage board I had made out of a piece of left-over bird's-eye maple. I then fumbled further back in the desk for a Bicycle Jumbo deck. It was hard to find a good deck that had all fifty-two without corners missing. Many decks were so old, nonslide-able, and very sticky, you felt like you should glove up before attempting to use, or even touch them.

George made himself a large mug of hot chocolate, found some stale Oreo cookies in a cupboard, no ants, proceeded to set the pegs up in the correct holes on the board. Greg didn't say a word. He didn't want, or need, anything. He just sat there waiting for us to gather, find a seat at the large conference table, and start in on a game.

He was watching George, who had taken out the cards from their blue cardboard package. George counted them one by one on the table. There were fifty-two. He then counted them a second time to be sure they were all there. Then he checked for jokers, none found. George was now just about to his final step. He started shuffling, and shuffling ... shuffled ... shuffled ... shuffled again ... shuffle ... shuffle ... shuffle ... Greg went from warm, to slow simmer, to rapid boil.

"PLAY!" Greg screamed. George jumped to

attention. We cut for deal—low card. Greg cut a four. George handed him the deck of blue cards. Greg started to deal out five cards each, with an extra for the crib.

"OK, all nickels dealt you, put in the crib, please," he said. Fat chance of that ever happening!

"OK, *Road Cone* ... you want to concede three games before we start, or do you want to see if you know how to play this game! Let me see, over fifty years you've been trying to learn, isn't it? Must be you can't read the rules, just look at the pictures!"

Ah yes, Wonderful Greg, he was always such a sweet fellow! I responded by giving him a one-finger salute.

I got the name *Road Cone* last winter. I was wearing a big yellow-orange Emergency Response coat I had just bought, on sale, at Job Lots. That, plus my bright orange winter knitted pull-down cap made me a real bright standout. We had been toned for a multi-car accident on I-91 in a snowstorm. When we arrived on the scene, C-3 yelled, "Jackman ... get out there! Be a Road Cone. Slow these suckers down before they really muck it up, make a total mess out of things!" From that day on ... *Road Cone* stuck like glue!

We played our first game. One time up the outside, first and second streets. Then back down the board on the inside track, third street, the skunk line, then fourth street. I didn't win the game. I wasn't even close. Greg came in second, I was third. If there were ten people playing, I'd come in twenty-sixth! ... Stupid game doesn't like me! We were counting our first hands of the second game.

"Eight," Greg said.

"I've got twelve, and the right jack," said George. "What you got, Jackman?"

"Four, nothing in the crib," I replied.

Really sad that some things never change. The front door opened, then closed with a clunk. The scent of pipe smoke came first, then Paul. He sort of silently sauntered in, blew a few puffs, pulled up a chair across from me, sat down. He smiled, slowly shaking his head back and forth.

"I knew it, Abe! You're a glutton for punishment! I think you'd be frozen by now ... losing your shirt so many times. You ever won a single game this year?"

How nice it was that Paul, plus everyone else in the world, knew my Dow Jones cribbage average was on a downward spiral. No one ever applauded whenever I actually won a game. Looking at the board, Greg was already ahead by two over George. I was seven behind George. Hey! ... It was early! ... I still had a chance! We were all close at the top of third street in our game, trying to make the skunk line, fourth street still to go, when the next tone for Westland came in.

"*Beep ... Beep ... Beep ... Beep* ... The tone is for Westland, suspected structure fire at 45 Old Oakwood Road, Westland West, the Porterson residence, nearest crossroad is Eagle's Nest Trail, west end .... for Westland, structure fire, 45 Old Oakwood Road, Westland."

CHAPTER 2

Paul Whipple is a good, close friend. He is one fellow I've known since dirt was invented. I'd worked with him a lot of different ways over the years. He has been our local constable just about as long as there have been clouds in the sky, or solid ground under your feet.

Laid-back isn't quite the right word for Paul. He is a listener, a thinker, a ponderer of thoughts. He doesn't say much—his pipe does most of his conversations without a word ever spoken. When he does talk, however, your ears better perk right up, almost strain yourself, to listen real good!

Paul has the last little farm on Whippletree Lane. Actually, it's not the last farm, it's the only farm on Whippletree. Brady Tuttle has about two acres on the corner of Whippletree, a good half mile from Paul's land. Tuttle has a small house with a three-car garage off to one side. Anyone asking directions to Paul's is told to turn just past Tuttle's. There are no street or lane signs to speak of. Everyone, of course, is expected to know exactly where Brady Tuttle lived. If you were one of those poor souls that had no clue who Brady Tuttle even was, or lived, you couldn't get there from here. Paul remained undisturbed.

Whippletree is a small dirt road to no place. A semi-private lane with a turnaround at the end. It's a little over a mile long. Paul's father dug, cleared, plowed, really cared about that plot of ground. He gave Whippletree Lane its pretty name. Old Man Whipple built the log cabin Paul, his dog Michelangelo, now resided in. Set it back a little, behind some high bushes, with a stone wall near the turnaround. It was a quiet place with a lot of trees, a small field, a brook, a small pond. The stream fed Paul's pond, then spilled over to meander through his wood lot, disappearing away as it went into deep woods.

Whipple's pond wasn't very large. Paul had built a small, mobile wooden dock. He'd use the dock during the summer months, then pull it out, cover it with a blue tarp, before the snows of winter came. The dock was only six feet long by five feet wide, as a guess. Good enough for a lawn chair with a makeshift shade umbrella, duct taped, above. Michelangelo had just enough room at Paul's feet to circle once, lay down to nap. Good place to read a book while enjoying a pipe.

The pond wasn't very deep either. Not really

deep enough to dive into. A few spots might touch on ten feet deep, but the norm wouldn't be much over the five-foot mark. It had cold, drinkable, clear water flowing through it all year. Frogs, tadpoles, salamanders, flitting dragonflies were all plentiful. If there were fish of any kind in the pond, they were few. A "brookie" might pass through once in a great while, but wouldn't set up shop. Too shallow for a good fishing ground.

Papa Whipple died in a logging accident about fifteen years ago. Paul liked quiet. Paul's dog Michelangelo, sleeping most of the time unless a visitor came by, liked quiet too. The end of Whippletree Lane was a nice quiet place most of the time. It was peaceful.

Me, I'm Abe Jackman. They call me the *Road Cone* on the Westland Fire Department. I am an old retired high school teacher. Lived here in Westland Village most of my life. I live with my wife, two cats, a few mice on occasion, squirrels, birds, and Salty. I've been an EMT, on our volunteer fire department, for over forty years. Over those years you get to know a lot of people. Being in a village, everyone here knows everyone, and most are related in some way.

When it comes to dogs, Paul's Michelangelo—Mike for short—is a riot. A four-year-old bloodhound—brown, black, white. His skin you could pull in any direction. The beast would never move his large frame or feet at all. That dog could stretch a foot in any direction you pulled without even a twitch. Amazing!

You had to be on guard for Mike's floppy mouth at all times. If the bounding hound, awakened from sleep by your coming into his presence, didn't lick you to death as a first greeting, he would then revert to the use of "Plan B." Skillfully pictured in his mind, honed down to perfection, Mike would sneak up on you. Within the next few minutes of your arrival, he would lay his giant head in your lap, begging for a good ear scratch.

Large pools of drool were forthcoming, soaking you down in friendship. That dog could really drool! He then would raise his head in a manly, high-society sort of way. Coming from the deep depths, way down inside, billowing to the surface, was heard a resounding "Aaahh-roooo."

It was a very distinctive sound! If you made the mistake of sitting down on the sofa when Mike was in view, you were very likely in trouble. Slowly sneaking over, inching closer to you, Mike would put his feet up in your lap. You were instantly pinned to the sofa. Just two innocent front paws up at first, then, slowly, methodically, a back foot ... *PLOP!* ... His body was on top of you. Had to be over seventy-five pounds of pure dog. Pull, tug, push as you might, the beast could not be budged from your lap. He was very comfortable there, would fall asleep, snore softly.

Paul would have to give Mike a special command if you wanted the beast moved. Once given, Mike would obey instantly, be off, looking about for other sleeping quarters. Horrors befell you if you forgot to wear a raincoat. You would be covered in saliva! "Salivate" was not one of Paul's dog commands. Mike would do it for you, free of charge, without being asked!

His nose! Did I mention Michelangelo's nose! A true bloodhound he was, that loved to sniff!

He would find chipmunks in a pile of leaves, frogs by the stream or pond, a scrap of cloth in a stone wall, or an old silver quarter dug up from the lawn. He would find anything!

A small painted turtle once met his acquaintance. Mike, quite puzzled, picked it up delicately in his massive mouth and deposited it at Paul's feet, unharmed. Mike looked up in wonder, asking, "What sort of strange rock have I found today? ..." Poor turtle looked up covered in drool! Very undignified. When put back near the pond, Mr. Turtle would make his escape into the cool water, clean himself off, then disappear under leaves at the bottom.

Mike was Paul's best friend. They were alike in many ways. They were both deep thinkers, head-scratchers, and on occasion, both liked a good nap. Paul would stretch out with a pillow and blanket on his large couch in the living room. Pipe smoked out, cleaned, close by in a green glass ashtray on the end table. Mike would cover Paul's feet, taking up the bottom half of the couch. It was a sight you had to get used to. Both of them snoring songs to each other.

When the two were awake, however, things were different. They both were very much on track—noses to the book or to the ground, as the case might be. Both always studying, sniffing out clues, pondering new ideas, adventures in the world around them.

Only difference between them was Paul's corn-cob smoking pipe. Mike knew the smell of it ... knew Paul was close by. It was a pity the dog never learned how to blow a smoke ring. Paul could, did often, with a twinkle in his eye. They were a good team nonetheless.

Paul, Mike, Salty with me, were three-day-a-week regs at the Paleyville Diner in Paleyville. The diner was the next town down from Westland. Go straight south on Route 45. The Paleyville Diner, just coming into the village, opened at five thirty for breakfast every morning.

There was "No Parking" on the right side of Route 45 as you came south into Paley Village. You had to turn into the old brick bank parking lot. The bank was on the right side, just past the diner. You swing a right angle, making a total "U-ee" around the bank, past the outside ATM. Then cut to the left, look both ways, put yourself back onto the left side of Route 45. If you managed it right, you would now be heading north, looking for an open space.

You needed to pray that there was one space left available to snuggle into. Parking was always a struggle. Sometimes you'd go around three, maybe four, times before a space opened up. It was a real merry-go-round at times. Very often, you would think a space was open, seeing a farmer pull out of one, heading back to the farm. Then, before you could make your move, some wiseass would drive right past you, pull in, park it. They never waited a bit! Thought nothing of it! Salty beside me, we would both growl.

You couldn't beat a farmer to breakfast in Paleyville. They were up before three, milking their blessed cows. This was hours before Salty or I started to wakie-wakie. They had priority parking over us late sleepers, usually stayed for more than one cup of coffee.

Most folks that came for breakfast knew each other either by face, name, or smell. We would chatter about the weather; a birthday coming up, or just past; someone's death that was usually expected, but unexpected when it actually happened.

"Yep, old whatziz-face was a helluva good

man. Cancer got him, you know. Poor fella, didn't stand a chance in hell. Smoked all the time, you know, pack a day. Yep, helluva good man he was. I'll miss the poor bastard!" On it went, different every morning.

Fishing, hunting—there was always something to shoot the morning breeze about. We stayed away from politics unless something really major was in the works. Those folks working in Washington have the world so screwed up we didn't want to talk about it, or even think how bad it's all getting. We don't want to discuss it much. Didn't want to screw things up even more!

Flatlanders were always good for a headache. You could always tell when one or more outside-down country folk stopped at the diner for breakfast. Never mattered who you were, they were there first, demanded attention. Pushy-shovey, "had to order before anybody else"-type folks. Then, they would expect breakfast to be served to them on gold platters four minutes ago. Annoying little buggers, some of them are!

Their time was much more valuable than your time. They always changed their minds four times while ordering. No manners to speak of. Their conversations were always quite loud. Everyone in the diner had to know every important word they spoke. From their booth in the corner comes "Precious, darling, Popsicle

Woodpile ... Do you have enough creamy-creamy for your coffee-woffie, darling?"

"Oh Freddie, you dashing silly boy. I only had seven individual creamers, darling. Could you ask for more please, Honey Poo? ... Real cream, darling, I don't think these little things they gave us, with the pull-off tops, will do at all. Thank you so much, Sweetie Pie."

It gets very sickening real quick. You really want to poke them with your fork, or use up good duct tape! Waste of good duct tape, but it would help to keep them quiet!

A few months ago one very obnoxious dweeb made the mistake of asking Dan Stoneman, a grainy true Vermont local, directions to some farm out in Westland West none of us ever heard of. Dan scratched his head a moment, then, with a twinkle in his eye, straightforward as could be, started right in with very well-rehearsed directions, made up as he went along. The poor fellow, directions all scribbled down, checked over twice, must have followed Dan's directions to the letter. Led the fool on a forty-mile snipe hunt in the wrong direction; must have seen a good half of southern Vermont by the time he ran out of gas. He has never been seen in Paleyville since that day.

Flatlanders are even worse on I-91. They think they own the road. You had better move aside pretty fast! Get out of their way, move it! It's always the other guy that can't drive at eighty-five in a blizzard!

"It's the damn car's fault it went off the road, Officer. You can't blame me, I was just driving. Just you look at this. It says it right here, in the manual I bought, from the Goofy Moose Auto Book Club. With two-year-old snow tires, I should, in a blinding blizzard, be able to get this baby up to a hundred miles an hour easy!"

They'll say it every time. Must be no-fault-for-dummies insurance, where they come from. You can learn, hear, observe a whole lot while eating breakfast at a diner. There is something new to chew on every day. On the interstate, you listen, look, learn survival skills! You have to!

CHAPTER 3

Kayle Central Dispatch had spoken! We had
a fire! I was actually winning! Cards went
flying on the table. George went for his turn-
out gear. Greg, with me close behind, bounded like jackrabbits for the dispatch office. C-3
signed on with us; he had already told Kayle he
was responding to our station. Greg told Kayle
Dispatch that Westland Dispatch was on the air.
We acknowledged that we heard the call. We
were now setting our ducks in a row to respond.

All four red doors went up one second after
the other. C-3 led the procession of pickups,
their lights ablaze, sirens going. All were flying down Fireman's Trail. There were squeals
of brakes, splashes of mud, truck doors flying
open, truck doors slamming shut. A lot of hus-
tle, bustle, then run.

Engine-3 was the first out the door, with
three aboard. Rescue-1 was close behind. The
first tanker rumbled out, turned toward Route
45. Platform-2 started its engine.

Dispatch was all chatter on our frequencies.

"C-3 to dispatch, did you tell Kayle we're responding?"

C-3 always wanted to know that Kayle knew we were on the road.

"Engine-3, I'm responding."

"Tanker-1, I'm gone."

More firemen, in their apparatus driver seats, waited for a break in the frequency chatter so they could say they were out the gate, responding.

We then heard Jon Stealman from West Station. West Station had one engine, one tanker housed outside the West village. A small station with just enough room to fit the two vehicles in if you didn't sneeze. It was just south of the village store, across from the old white one-room schoolhouse, next to where the old Congregational church had been that burned down in the seventies. The volume was weak—very scratchy, but readable.

"Kayle, this is Engine-1. I'm responding from the West," Jon said. "I can see the smoke from it, from the station. As I remember it, it's a big house. We might want a second alarm ..." Then more chattering cut in, drowning out anything else said from the West.

"Rescue-1 has responded, did you tell Kayle yet?"

"Tanker-2, responding."

"Tanker-3, responding."

"Platform-2's out the door."

"C-3 to dispatch, did you tell Kayle we're responding yet?"

"C-2 to C-5, I'll pick you up on my way to the station."

"C-5 on, got it, C-2. Thanks. I'll be out at the road."

Everyone had to get in an important word about something! We had called Kayle Central Dispatch, on our landline, long ago. When all is yack, on all frequencies, a landline usually worked to get through to Kayle.

Engine-3, along with Rescue-1, were the first two units called into Central Dispatch. A minute later, we had called a second time. We told Kayle the rest of our cavalry was out the door responding as well.

Trouble was, C-3 can't hear it if we use landline. If C-3 didn't hear it, accordingly, a sound was never made from our dispatch office. The assumption was then made that Kayle was never notified. Mother Hen #3 would then get very nervous very quickly, thinking we had left Central Dispatch in the dark. Greg reached C-3 on his cell phone and informed him Kayle Dispatch was notified. They were well aware of all our apparatus that had responded. C-3 could stay calm!

Kayle Dispatch asked if we wanted a second alarm. I radioed C-1.

"Might not be a bad idea" was his answer. C-1 wasn't close to the scene as yet. Jon Stealman, on Engine-1, said it looked like it had a good head start on us. The smoke rise he could see from a half mile away was big, boiling into the windy sky. We were asking Kayle for a second alarm as Engine-1, with Jon speaking, came on the air.

"E-1, I'm on the scene. We have a fully in-volved, three-story house fire. Can see flame coming from all sides, all floors. She is really cooking! The barn is in close proximity to the house. No flames showing from the barn, that I can see."

His message was to the point, businesslike, almost calmly spoken—that was Jon. The second alarm soon went to a third. Riverdale came up with their engine to cover our station in case we had another call of some kind. All of Paleyville Fire & Rescue went directly to the scene. Seven other stations responded to the fire. Some de-partments covered different stations. Others were sent to the scene, mostly with tankers for the water supply. Three engine companies were sent to the scene. Our Platform-2 was there, set up with two engines supplying it water from a porta-tank.

The weather called for more snow. The temperature was dropping rapidly. Within an hour our station thermometer read 11 degrees

Fahrenheit, down from 18 a half hour earlier. The wind had picked up, too. It was slowly getting dark, cold, miserable outside.

Snow was now blowing around. Starting as a few flurries of flakes, now changing to coming down steadily. The stiff cold wind started pushing harder, telling us Mother Nature wasn't finished with winter this evening, as yet. She still had a few tricks in store for us to brave through.

Greg, with me beside, both worked dispatch until radio traffic settled down. I started making coffee, then checked with our women's auxiliary, by landline, to see what could be done for sandwiches. They were way ahead on me. When a few ladies had heard what we had on their home scanners, the sandwich patrol rolled into action. Sandwiches were on their way. They would come to the station, all boxed neatly, wrapped individually. We then trucked out a wide assortment of foods, snacks, hot or cold drinks, to distribute to those working at the scene.

Two hours into the call, darkness was upon us. It was cold, dark black, windy with blowing snow, now coming down hard. Not the best night to be out in boots, layers of clothes, turnout gear, fighting a major fire with a wet hose line in your gloved hands!

There wasn't much squawk in the dispatch office. Many were still very busy on the scene trying to save the red barn, and what little was left of the house. They didn't have the time to chatter with the likes of us. I went out, packed the RAV-4 with four boxes of the various sandwiches, soda, water, candy bars. Next came four large 20-cup coffee containers, cups, half and half, sugar and other condiments. With all packed in so nothing would fall over, I was ready to embark westward bound.

I raced the RAV's engine a few seconds more, trying to feel some warmth coming from the vents in a very cold car interior. I turned on my seat heater, buckled up, headed across Route 45, down Fletcher Street to the end, turned left toward the hills. The roads were slick. I tracked up over the mountain toward the scene of the fire in Westland West. God that wind was strong! It was rocking the car every few seconds.

I could smell the smoke long before I was ever close to getting to the fire scene. Paul was there directing traffic. Mike stayed home asleep. That is one smart dog! Paul's pipe was going like a Stanley Steamer. He was standing—an Eskimo in lime green. He was all bundled up, directing at the junction in the road where it looped back onto itself. He had a wand flashlight, was directing tankers in, then out from a porta-tank water-drop zone. The porta-tank would have been the first thing tankers would have set up when first arriving. It would be on the side of the road, out of the way of engines, but as near as possible to the house fire.

Paul had made a nice one-way loop. All traffic in one way, out the other. It worked well if everyone went the right way. You had to be patient, sometimes wait a while, and always listen to what Paul had to say.

Paul was very patient, but if you didn't listen, went your way instead of the right way, well, golly whiskers, guess what just got all screwed up! Paul would be on you like a tick on a hound. You might be lucky to just get yelled at. If you really tangled things up, a fifty-dollar fine, possibly more, came attached to his yelling at you.

Paul didn't get rich. It was one of Paul's learning tools. The guilty party that lost a few farthings learned quickly from a hole in his pocket! It was thought that lightning bolts would flash out of the sky, striking you down instantly, if you didn't follow Paul's directions to the letter.

He was a tough old bird. As an officer of the law, he demanded respect, got it always. No one ever tried to mess with Paul! He was right, guilty party wrong! That was the end of the story! Pull out your wallet!

Traffic worked like a well-oiled machine when Paul was in charge. He would twirl his baton, and all came to attention. All companies worked well together, both at the scene or covering stations. They made good music. Near

Paul, however, each passing all got puffs of pipe smoke in our faces.

"Coffee, sandwiches, Paul. Where do you want them?"

"Pull up behind your Engine-3, we'll use the back for a table, unload what you got."

I pulled up to the right of the engine, off the road as much as I could push. I didn't realize how cold it was until I opened the car door. A blast of snow hit me in the face; bitter cold wind was close behind.

Damn! ... I zipped my coat tighter, pulled up my scarf, put on my gloves. I unpacked the RAV, started some milling firemen toward coffee, doughnuts, sandwiches of all kinds. Two or three shivering figures that found coffee turned into a dozen quickly. Once they knew what was where, they figured how to quickly get hot coffee to their mouths; standing ice cubes started to melt a little bit. I started sorting, planning what I could carry. I took a thermos, cups, a plastic creamer bottle, of course a large bag of doughnuts—that should do it for the first run. I headed toward the glow fifty yards ahead on the road, arms full of goods.

The house was still burning, not much left of it. Total loss. One wall standing, teetering when a hose line's blast hit it. There were some low flames still to be put out, but mostly everything was under control. Two-and-a-half-inch hose lines were spraying from the back. You could make out silhouettes in the darkness when lights, on apparatus, flashed, lighting them up for a moment.

Platform-2 had a lazy stream coming down. Its tower was stationed at the front corner of the house. The barn showed a few scars on the near side, burned just slightly, mostly cosmetic. Ninety-five percent of her was still up, old but good, unscathed from the dying inferno that had been fairly close next door. No farm stock had been in the barn, thank goodness.

The coffee went fast. Rick Davis, with George Kratcher beside him, were on the hose lines on the back side of the burning structure. I came up to them with cups of steaming coffee, a half-full bag of doughnuts. Rick's face had a few white splotches on his nose. His cheeks had white, red-edged, quarter-sized marks as well. I noticed both quickly when I walked up to him with coffee in my hand. He was shivering badly. He gladly accepted the cup of coffee I handed him. Rick had all the signs of early-stage frostbite. It needed to be treated quickly before it got any worse. George had been taught to look out for frostbite signs. He should have seen the signs on Rick's face.

"Damn it, George ... You're supposed to watch for this!" I barked.

George looked up from his steaming coffee cup.

"Whaaa," he said, mouth full of doughnut. He quickly washed it down with two glugs of coffee. He grabbed a second doughnut.

"Whazzah matter, wha' did I do?"

I saw Bill Smith, an inside man from the Charlmont Department, standing by a hose line that was shut down. He was holding the nozzle, keeping it off the snow-covered ground. He found a good place to leave his hose, safe, to come over to help out. He took over for Rick. Bill was in need of coffee, which I got him with a doughnut. He was cold but doing alright.

"Get yourself back to Blue Angel," I said. "Let Wanda take a look at you. Your face is getting too cold.."

"I'm OK. It's nothing. I'm just cold, that's all," Rick answered.

"No, Rick, you've got early frostbite signs ... move yer butt!"

Sorry, rookie. You're not getting by me on this one! I'm an EMT-Basic. I look for danger signs all the time. Rick's face stood out like a picture in a manual: Frostbite, Chapter 9, Picture #2. I led Rick down through the puddles, many small streams of dirty water, to the Blue Angel—A-3—ambulance. It was parked back a ways, on the main road, out of trouble.

I think Wanda Fitzpatrick was happy to get some action. She put Rick sitting in back, on the cot. It was a nice warm ambulance. Rick was still a shaking bowl of Jell-O. Now his face started to hurt, as the warm replaced the cold. He was about to rub his cheeks. Wanda stopped him quickly. Rubbing the cheeks vigorously at that time was not a good thing to do! Not when cheeks are in that condition. Rubbing would damage the skin more. Wanda was a good paramedic. She knew what to do, or not do. Rick was in good hands.

I went back to Engine-3. The tail of the engine, where I set up, was a mess. I started to clean up. Empty thermos bottles drained of coffee, used cups, empty creamers, wrappers, soda cans, napkins, water bottles were scattered about here and there. No food of any kind was left at all! That was all long gone!

I put the boxes, containers, all other implements of debris or destruction that I had gathered into the car. I slowly turned my buggy around, straightened her out, back onto the dirt road. I headed for the main blacktop, covered with snow, back over the hills to our main station. Plow had been through recently, so the road wasn't too bad. Blue Angel ambulance passed me coming down the front side of the mountain. Lights were on, no siren, going fairly slow. They didn't seem to be in any big hurry to get to wherever. They had someone in the back. I suspected it was Rick.

Someone would be at the fire scene all night.

A good water supply would be handy. Most everyone else returned to their respective stations by midnight, or a little after. From their stations, they eventually headed home to a few hours' sleep.

We had lights on the scene, but it had already been a hard night. It was decided Mop Up operations would continue in the next morning, early. No one had been home, or around the place, when the fire started. At least no one that we knew of.

CHAPTER 4

Morning came way too early. Salty was eager to go out, find some sticks to chew apart, do his usual morning constitutional. Face licking started promptly at 6:30 A.M. I slowly moved from warm bed to feet on cold floor. I mumbled a few incoherent words, headed toward the bathroom. Mr. Bleary-eyed Fuzz-face let the Salt out the front door to romp around, do his "I found a branch" dance. He then, finally, with a lot of coaxing from the peanut gallery, proceeded to pee and poop. I got cleaned up and dressed. I took my morning pills, had OJ, a bowl of Granola Crunches, an English muffin. I was good to go.

Salty was fed, ate it all in seconds, now eager to go someplace. I got my camera, checked the battery, bundled up, opened the front door for Salty. We both headed for the car. Salty, as co-pilot, had his head out the window, tongue flapping as we went along. He didn't last long. Head came back in quickly. Cold! I closed his window. I could feel the cold wind on the back of my neck with it open.

We headed toward West-West to check the goings-on. The road over had three inches of snow covering it, and was very slippery. I could see where two unknowns had slip-slided away. They had gone off the road into the pucker brush. One on one side, one on the other. Both had enough back-out power to get themselves pushed back on the road, continue on to places far and away.

Mop Up was way ahead of us timewise. Salty, with me driving, didn't leave our house until a little past seven. It was slow going to get up over the hills to West-West. When we finally did arrive on scene, Paul was there ahead of us. Mike was there, too.

I could see George with his pipe pole poking about on the far side of the interior. There was a haze of lingering smoke mixed with cold morning fog. Over on the right side of the rubble, about halfway back where the kitchen used to be, yellow tape was stretched.

It ran square across that specific section of remaining house, continued out five or six feet from the side of the house to what earlier had been the snow-covered side lawn. Now all that was seen there was charred remains with sooty, ash-covered mush, footprints, dirty puddles of water, a single, uncharged hose line running through on the ground. All remaining reminders of the night before.

"What's that all about?" I asked. Paul took a long puff of smoke.

"Oh, they found something. We had to cordon it off. We don't want that area to be disturbed."

Paul then explained it all to me slowly. George Kratcher had started Mop Up, with his pipe pole, about two hours earlier. Very methodical, George had worked slowly back one way, then forth, starting from the front right corner. He worked inch by inch forward. He had hit on something he thought was an oblong bottle, down under a burned piece of second flooring that had fallen. It was in the kitchen area. Found it right up next to the gas stove, about where the kitchen table, chairs, roll-around, used to be.

Paul continued, "Well, you know George is a good poker. Not going to find a bottle, leave it unturned you know. He'd been digging around a good twenty minutes or so, before he stumbled onto it. Really burned up pretty good, all black and all. 'Course he found out quick, it wasn't a bottle. No, Sir! George kept poking. It was down in there pretty good. He pried it loose from under a few burned-up boards on top, and all." Paul took a pause.

"Well, Kratcher pulled it up with his pole, turned it over. Sure enough, there it was. Somebody's burnt skull looking straight up at him. Damn! It sure did shake him up a bit! Rest of the body is down under there too. Not much left to see. Don't want it to be moved until the big boys get here."

Paul took his beloved pouch out of his green plaid vest, stuffed, lit his pipe with a fresh fill.

"Kind of puts a new twist on things," he said.

He blew a large smoke ring, let it drift quickly down the field.

"Say, you aren't up to much right now, are you? You, with Salty there, want to do me a favor?"

"What is it?" I asked.

"Medical examiner's due here in a half hour. I don't want anyone snooping around here, messing stuff up before he gets here. I got a few people that I'll let stay: George, the captain, the two chiefs are OK, but the rest don't need to be here, squirtin' hoses, messing about. The rest of these yahoos are leaving—right now! Once out, nobody in!"

He looked around, cleared his throat, spit in the snow. The constable continued, "I need you to go out to the end of Oakwood. Anything wanting to come this way, turn 'em around. Tell them to go the other way. No one down the road at all. No, Sir—not one single soul! Let the examiner through, 'course, but no one else, at all! Firemen, gawkers, hillbillies—kick them all out! God knows, the damn press will show up. Nobody gets down here, you got it?"

He finished with another two puffs of smoke,

now curling around my face. That was Paul's way of adding another exclamation point to what was just said. He walked back to his cruiser.

I grabbed four large orange cones from a stack left near Paul. I had enough to help me block the road, put them in the way. Salty was getting excited—he knew something was going on. It didn't matter what it was. He had a sixth sense when something was happening.

When we reached the end of Oakwood, I parked the car at a forty-five-degree angle across the right side of the road. I had my red lights on. My RAV-4 blocking half the entrance onto Old Oakwood. Then placing four cones close together across the rest of the entrance, about a foot or more apart—no vehicle could get through. The road was blocked all the way across. Nothing could go through without nailing at least one or two cones in the process. The road was blocked off in good order.

Salty, on a long, spring-loaded coil leash, stood guard with me. Salty liked being out on the leash. It gave him a feeling of importance. We turned around a few sightseers. Salty got to lick a few hands. We had a few would-be helpers from different departments show up. They were told they could return to their departments. No they couldn't go down, look around. One engine, with three firemen, left the scene, headed home. They presumably left from Paul's commanding them to do so. Salty stayed put while I moved the cones out of the way, letting them be on their way. Then I moved cones back into place. Salty decided to hop back into the car. It was cold. The car was warm.

We had been at our post for about twenty minutes when an older jet-black, wing-tailed caddie pulled up to a stop. The driver rolled down his window.

"Hi! ...Wilton Press here ... This where the fire was?" he asked.

He had a green button-down shirt with a V-neck sweater. An overcoat was on the seat next to him.

"Correct, Sir, but the road is closed to all traffic. No one can go down," I answered.

"I'm the press," he shouted, "I have a story to cover."

"Can't go down, sorry."

"Who the hell are you? Who's in charge around here?"

"I'm in charge right here. Sorry, Sir. You can't go."

"You aren't the Chief. Chief said I could go!"

"Sorry, Sir, no one goes down."

"Go down there right now! Get your chief right up here! I'm the press, I have a right!"

"No."

"Can't get there at all then, huh."

"That's right."

"Would you take a twenty?"

"No."

"I'll park it over there, walk on down, then."

"No you won't!"

"What? I can't take my camera bag. Walk it?"

"No, you can't."

"I suppose you think you're going to stop me."

"There are two state policemen, a constable, me with my dog in the car, all here to stop you. I wouldn't try to force the issue. I'm fairly sure you wouldn't get far. It wouldn't be in your best interest to be arrested, spend some jail time, pay a fine. All that, before you got halfway there."

On we went, back and forth, for a good forty-five minutes. Salty started barking at him, very concerned, in the back seat of the car. I thought he had finally given up. He blew out a loud breath, shrugged his shoulders, then opened up a briefcase on the seat next to him.

"Can't go down at all? This fireman's a tough nut to crack!" he muttered under his breath.

He straightened up, held his hand out the window.

"Here!"

Flap, flap, flap, flap ..... at least twenty identification cards trickled down from plastic folders from his open window. He had this silly grin, from ear to ear, on his face.

"Fred McCarthy, Sir, Medical Examiner.

You keep up the good work. Good job!! Can I go through now, please?"

That son of a ... I was tempted to sic Salty on him. Have him thoroughly licked to death! Reluctantly, I moved the cones over, let him move on with his *"Get Out of Jail Free"* cards still intact.

"Oh! If the hearse shows up, could you let those boys through, please? Keep the rest of the lovers out of Lovers' Lane, though ..... Good job!"

The Lone Ranger drove on down the road in a cloud of muddy slop!

"Hi Yo Cad-Diddly, Away!"

He was out of sight. I looked at the bright side. Paul had trained me well. A good guess told me the examiner's test, which I'd completed in just under an hour, was passed with flying colors!

CHAPTER 5

There was the usual hustle-bustle at the station. Trucks to clean, hose lines to wash, hang, many air packs to de-con, fill correctly. Greg Dagnaski was away from dispatching, rolling cleaned hose coming down from the tower. Seventeen clean dry lengths came down on pulleys from the top, making room for the mass of freshly washed inch-and-a-half. House fires used up a lot of hose pretty quickly. There was always a commander barking for another line, to another location, early into a fire scene. We had the back of the utility piled high with wet ash-covered spools, still dripping gray water.

Dirty hose lines would be rolled all the way out a bay door. Then, starting at one end, they were slowly run through the washer. Many times the hose lines had to be scrubbed down even more, or run through the hose washer a second time. It wasn't easy trying to make them look good again.

Wet hose, cleaned off as best as possible, was then divided in half. It would be pulled over to whoever was the rope man in the tower. The hose tower was at the back of the station. Once the hose tower door was opened, the inside tower, going up three stories, had over thirty doubled, heavy-duty rope lines, all hanging down.

They were all rigged by pulleys at the top of the tower. A rope line went up, was threaded through, then came back down: one continual circle of rope. A two-foot length of spliced-in rope, with an "s" hook, was spliced in at the middle dividing line of each double rope line in question. Each was fastened securely to a cleat on the wall at the bottom.

An unused rope would be unfastened from its cleat. The two-foot length then wrapped around a wet hose, fastened with the "s" hook securely. Up the hose would go! The rope man pulling the other free line tautly down, bringing the "s"-hooked hose to the top. Both ends of the hose, hopefully, dangled off the floor, dripping. The heavy-tension rope line that had been pulled down would then be guided to a free cleat on the tower wall, fastened securely. It, usually, next to several other taut lines from other hose lines drying. The tower was hardly ever empty.

Next! Another waiting hose line, freshly run through the washer, would be divided, then wrapped twice around with rope, hooked correctly with the "s" hook. Now ready, it would be pulled to the tower top to join others dripping down. The tower man or anyone close by him had to be careful, alert at all times. A careless hook of the "s," a badly tied rope to a cleat, or an unattended taut line could result in a heavy hose coming down. It happens, but not too often.

J.J. Adams was washing down the Rescue. Others were restocking, checking their chore lists twice. It takes time before all is back in order, packed up, and clean. Once all trucks were packed correctly, all gear cleaned, back on board in the right places, all truck reports filled out, signed, turned in, Greg or whoever was dispatching could call us in.

The dispatcher would tell Kayle Central Dispatch everything was "hunky-dory" in Westland world. We had all things back in station, back in service. Of course, we would get another call just as soon as we told Kayle everything was all set. We would get toned right on time, have to take the Rescue with an engine to something, get all things all dirty again. It was the name of the game.

We got the word that Rick Davis was OK. He spent the night at the hospital. They let him loose in the morning with pills, goo for his face, instructions on how to take care of himself. The frostbite on his face was minor. The face would hurt as the circulation slowly came back to the damaged skin. He was a little discolored, but he was going to survive in one piece.

The nurses found out his feet were all waxy as well. Soon as they took his boots off at the hospital, they realized his feet were wet, cold, not looking their best. Summer lightweight ankle socks in wet boots. He was lucky. It could have been much worse. He didn't use his face glove or face shield as he had been instructed to do so, either. The Chief was unsympathetic, said he'd learn the hard way. Hopefully Rick learned. It won't happen again any time soon.

It was Friday morning before I saw Paul again. He came in, sat down in his usual seat across from me at Paley's, blew some smoke in my face. We got over two feet of snow from Tuesday night late on through to Wednesday evening. Clung to all the trees. It was a pretty Winter Wonderland outside all day Wednesday. It was pretty this morning, driving down to breakfast with Salty.

Last two days were stay-at-home, stay-warm days. Hunker down with a log or two in the wood stove, watch the white stuff blow by the windows. It came down pretty good for a while there. Good nap weather. I'm sure Paul and Mike took advantage of it. I know Salty and I did. We had our own couch in our living room, too. It was across from a small wood stove with a large stone mantle behind. Nice to have a good fire going, hear the crackles, pops. Watch the fire creep up between the logs, fall asleep with the warmth, sounds of the fire.

Salty has a long, good history of snoring. Only dog I know that would sleep totally on his back, front paws in praying position, back legs stretched out. His snoring would wake me up every so often. His must be louder than mine. At least he didn't pig the quilt I usually had over me.

"So, what's the latest?" I asked Paul.

I'd put an order of blueberry pancakes, bacon, small OJ, in with Molly. She was putting a napkin, silverware down on the red-checked tablecloth for Paul. She looked the table over quickly. Salt and pepper, ketchup, a wire tray of small individual jams-jellies. It all checked out. She went to the kitchen window to put our orders in, came back with a small bowl of creamers for the coffee she had served us.

"Nothing." ... A curl of smoke.

"Fred, those boys of his, have the body at their lab someplace up north ... Female ... not that old, they thought. Fire marshall with some State boys have been around, looking at things again. That's it." ... A smoke ring slowly curled toward the ceiling.

"Can't say we've heard of anyone missing, we know of, yet."

He put two creamers in his coffee, took a small sip.

"They make a good cup of coffee here, don't they. Damn hot, though."

"A facing in stone. An embankment. It's got nine letters!" ... She was at it again.

"'Revetment.'" ... Another smoke ring.

"You got it. Fits right in. Thank you ..... Diminish, or shrink .... Oh, I got it, 'dwindle.'" ... On she went.

My blueberry pancakes came. I saved a piece of bacon in a napkin for my copilot. We chewed some more fat, mostly over the three-car accident they had on the interstate a few nights back. Two vehicles on their roofs. Front vehicle lost control on some ice. The car behind nailed it, going a pretty good clip at the time. They both went airborne, flipped over. Had to use "the Jaws" to get one couple out. One DOA, three critical. Had four ambulances on the scene. Took one by helicopter.

I was glad we didn't have to go. Accident was too far north of us, on the interstate. Skiers from down south, I expect. They fly low, zip along too fast, have to get to the slopes from cities afar. Many times they fall asleep. Too tired after driving three or more hours to where they were going. That, or they wanted to get there in two hours. Their trip, at the normal speed limit, should be a four-hour trip at best.

Maybe down south, the road conditions are that much better. It's pretty doubtful. Mother Nature has a nasty habit of stopping traffic—very quickly—when road conditions around here are all ice.

Nothing more about the fire out in West-West. Nothing about the body that was found. No new news, talk, information at all. Wasn't a thing new to say about any of it. I finished off my pancakes with a second cup of coffee. Paul had left ahead of me. I was out the door, back to the car, bacon in hand, five minutes after Paul. By the time I'd turned the key to start the engine, two pieces of bacon had disappeared from the seat next to me. We headed home.

CHAPTER 6

Paul, Mike, Abe, Salty went out to Old Oakwood Road Saturday morning. The snow, from days before, had melted down quite a bit near the fire scene. There was still a good, crusted covering. You could see there were a lot of footprints, zigzagging ATV tracks, snowmobile trails around the place. It was a bright, sunny day—a good day for a lot of snow to hopefully go away.

Mike was down, out of the back seat, with his nose to the ground. He was sniffing all tracks, pawing a few places, tail straight up, wagging. He was on the hunt! Paul was pondering. You could almost see the wheels slowly turning in his head. The internal computer was now turned on, quickly warming up.

Paul noticed little things that most others would pass right over, thinking nothing about them. We were standing on the remains of the kitchen floor. It was still pretty much intact. Burnt-through boards in places, they were heavy, thick planks before the fire. They could still hold our weight. Two boards had burned through completely. The boards were near what was once a fairly new gas stove, the front left corner of the stove tilted slightly into a hole where the floorboards used to be.

Paul had his hand on his pipe in thought; he had stopped puffing, was staring intently at the darkened metal stove. There were wrinkles on his forehead that meant he had puzzle pieces going on in his mind—big or little puzzle pieces that hadn't fit together yet.

"Humph." The cob puffed. "They're all off," Paul said, half to himself.

"What's off?" I asked him.

"Stove … Two burners were on after the fire. I'm sure of it. No gas left to speak of, of course, but I'm sure these two burners were on. Funny that someone would turn them off now. Don't think anyone's gonna be cooking anything on them too soon."

It was a little thing. To Paul, a little thing was a puzzle piece. It might just be a clue to something.

Mike was out in the snow. He had pawed a few spots, continued on, stopped, sniffed, continued on some more. He was on to a clue as well—he was sure something was there. Whatever it was, was on the other side of the yellow "*Do Not Cross*" tape, flapping from the stake ten feet out from the kitchen area. He kept coming back to the same spot, would paw a second, then let out with a resounding "AaaaaahRooo."

"Found something to play with, Sniffer Boy?"

Paul, with me two feet behind, stepped carefully over the edge of the house to where Mike had his head in a snow hole he had made. Paul reached into his vest, pulled out an old large metal spoon. That spoon was a significant item in Paul's assortment of tools he'd bring along on many an occasion. The spoon had helped Paul—Mike as well—dig a lot of little holes. Paul's spoon was just helping speed things up. Mike let us look in his hole. Nothing. At least nothing I saw, just more snow.

Paul bent down, started digging in Mike's hole with the serving spoon. When he stopped, Mike inspected the hole again. Nose went in deep, sniffing.

"AaaahRoo."

Mike spoke up, approving of Paul's progress. Paul got down on his knees at this point, busily tossing snow from the spoon carefully to one side. Mike's nose was never wrong. The dog wanted him to keep going.

"Humph. Found something down here," he said.

Mike was helping. Paul sat back on his knees, letting Mike have a go at digging. A minute later Mike deposited his find at Paul's kneecaps. A shell casing, very small, most likely a .22 long.

There were two of them buried down there that Michelangelo found, gave to Paul. Hell of a nose on that beast!

Maybe they meant something, maybe not. Paul put the shell casings both into a plastic sandwich bag. He always came prepared, stuffed the bag into his vest pocket.

Paul had noticed something else while milling about the place. One of the ATVs that had been passing by, circling around, had a gouge out of one tire. It was a very noticeable mark in the snow, if you were looking for that sort of thing. Paul had a sharp eye. Again, maybe nothing, maybe not. Paul added it to his puzzle pieces.

By the following Wednesday, nothing else was new. No clues at all on the female's identity. Paul, with the Vermont State Police, had tried to locate the Portersons—the owners of the charred remains of a farmhouse. It was found out they were out-of-state folks from New Jersey. The Portersons only used the place for ski weekends. At present, all anyone had found out was they were skiing some place out west, couldn't be reached.

Our first revaluation came from the Paleyville Diner a few days later. The two of us were in our usual booth munching away, drinking coffee. That's when Roscoe Billings, in the booth across from us, leaned over to ask us something.

"You boys talking about the fire out on Old Oakwood Road? ... I don't think the Portersons own that property anymore."

Roscoe was a well dressed, portly local realtor.

"Pretty sure they sold that about three, or four, months ago," he stated.

Aha! ... A news flash! ... A light dawning on yonder beak! That old cob was puffing in good shape now!

"Yes, I'm sure it was sold." Roscoe went back to his breakfast.

After a few long visits, phone calls, meetings on the street, look-ups at town offices, listers' offices, Paul had become a little more informed. A sale had taken place, both out of state, down a ways; also in state, but not quite as far away. Some lawyers, with real-estate people in attendance, knew about the sale. Some were present when it took place. Trouble was, no one near Westland would have heard a thing about it. Everything took place fifty miles away. If our town offices didn't get the message, our lister's office wouldn't have a clue; therefore no updates of a sale were in any files in Westland. This is a common occurrence in any Vermont small town, when town business is done elsewhere, without our officials in our town offices having any knowledge of it. The property in question now belonged to a Lapan family from Scotch Plains, New Jersey.

Our end of the line, from different angles, agencies, officials, had tried to contact them. No luck at all. Where the Lapan family was, was anybody's guess. Their phone was never answered. The Vermont State Police finally got in touch with one of their neighbors. The neighbor gave them some information that shed a small amount of light. The Lapan family was with friends down in the Florida Keys, vacationing. No, they had no idea of what their return date would be, or the names of the friends they were with. At least a slow start in the right direction.

CHAPTER 7

"*Beep ... Beep ... Beep ... Beep ......* The tone is for ..."

I was eating a late snack at the kitchen table. I filled my mouth with two remaining chocolate-chip cookies, took a swig of milk, got up from the table, grabbed my car keys. I didn't wait for the rest of the tone. I'd figure it out when I got to the station. I grabbed my gear, headed for the car, took off out the driveway toward the fire station.

I lived a short distance from the station, so it didn't take me long to get there.

"You go with Rescue, Jackman. Bad accident on 91, three cars with entrapment, mile south in the northbound."

I hopped into the back of the Rescue, seat-belted myself in, clipped a bungee cord to the door handle so there would be no chance of a surprise back-door opening en route. Rescue-1 with Engine-3 blew out of the station, guns blazing, lights on, siren wailing—here we go!

C-1 went direct, C-3 drove the Rescue with George beside him. Don't know who was in the engine. All I knew was the driver on Engine-3 told dispatch they had a full crew, they were responding. Accident was south of town on I-91. Close to the Paleyville line, but enough into Westland to make it ours. Sounded like a good one, at least three vehicles involved, Kayle Dispatch informed us. We passed the accident going south. One ambulance, with the state police, was already on the scene. We then went across the median, a mile further down, at the emergency U-turn, to go north to the accident. Traffic was starting to back up as we approached the scene. Blue Angel already had an ambulance on the scene; there was a second coming up behind our Engine-3. The Vermont State Police had two units there, with a third unit on its way. Paul was there, too.

C-3 angled Rescue-1 half into the breakdown lane, behind the accident, came to a stop. Ice-covered road! We were all bailing out on the guardrail side, if possible.

"*Road Cone*, get out there with some cones. Do your thing," screamed C-3.

I had piled out of the back, three cones in hand. I could see at least ten medical jackets, fifty feet up, at the accident. My medical skills up there could wait for the time being.

I started closing down the passenger lane. I laid cones out three feet apart at an angle from the guardrails in the breakdown lane, north, out to the midline of the highway. I stopped where the start of the high-speed lane began. More help arrived. I took at least a dozen yellow-or-ange cones from our utility truck. I put them out a foot apart in the closed passenger lane, angling cars toward the one open high- speed lane. This was the only lane open northbound to traffic. High speed, however, was now quickly diluted to low speed.

We thought we had the traffic pretty much under control. There were the cones, Engine-3's back yellow flashers directing the way, angled from half-passenger, half-breakdown lanes. Rescue-1, a state police vehicle, Utility-1 all came next with emergency lights on. They were all angled toward the breakdown lane. There had to be at least one hundred lights—red, yel-low, blue, flashing.

Twenty-five feet past our Utility-1 was the accident itself. Past the accident, a state police car, a second ambulance, Paul's cruiser, a sec-ond state police vehicle. This place was really lit up with emergency vehicle lights.

I was down with the cones. I had a foot-long "Darth Vader" lantern with a long, bright, glow-ing orange tube. We had a few flares out, stuck into the guardrails on the side. I was waving light traffic into the other lane ten feet before the start of the cones. As soon as I saw head-lights coming up over the rise coming north, I'd direct them over to the other lane. Everyone was slowing down, all going by without incident. There were a few small backups when traffic got heavier, but most of the time the left-lane north was flowing smoothly, slowly, or clear.

Four cars crested the rise. One moved over, two followed, three followed. My direction beam was working well. The number-four vehicle, however, was still in the passenger lane. It didn't bother me at first. Whoever it was, was still a goodly distance away. He had plenty of time to move over to the other lane. For whatever reason, the car kept coming.

I knew he must be able to see me. He had to see there was an accident ahead. He didn't budge from the passenger lane—he kept right on coming at a pretty good clip. Now he was close! Ten yards from me, I bounded over the guardrails. I did a belly flop into a snow bank. Two yellow reflective cones went flying up into the air. The car was weaseling its way down the breakdown lane.

"*Look out! ... One coming!*" I screamed toward the front of Engine-3.

Luckily, someone up there saw him coming, gave warning. I doubt anyone could have heard me screaming from that distance. Diesel engine noise would have drowned me out, easily.

Luckily, the next car coming north on the interstate came to a halt. Cones in front of him were flying in all directions over the road. I saw this kid, in a backward, dark-colored baseball cap with a long white, numbered football shirt, fly past. He was a teenager—looked young, anyway. He went by me quickly, in a two-seated sports buggy, down the breakdown lane.

Having destroyed the cone barrier, he proceeded to bump the guardrails on one side, scraping against the front bumper of Engine-3 on the other. It was a tight squeeze. He continually scraped the guardrails on his right side. He attempted to touch his brakes at that point, then gunned it past Rescue-1.

Just clearing the Rescue, he managed to put a small, fresh coat of green paint on his driver-side door. This was accomplished by passing the Vermont State Police cruiser just a mite too close. The car then passed Utility-1. He did turn on his blinker to signal after just passing U-1. A sharp left turn was taken, then a sharp right. The second turn, without signaling, put him into the high-speed lane. Rescue workers, firemen, police—all were scattering in many directions. All were trying to get out of his way.

The sports car then passed the actual accident, passed state police vehicle #2, the second ambulance, and Paul's cruiser. The kid driving just about reached state police cruiser #3 when he saw the two police officers waving him down.

He couldn't understand it, for the life of him!

Why would Paul, with a young state trooper, be standing near the high-speed lane, partially blocking his way? Why would they be in his lane of travel, trying to direct him to stop?! The car's brakes were finally applied—quickly. Paul took his hand off his revolver, clicked the strap back down.

Paul was not a happy camper. He had on his "Smokey the Bear," which he straightened, tipped down a hair in front. It became training day for the young trooper Joe next to him.

Paul walked up slowly to the vehicle in question, his hand on the strap of his revolver case, cold stare. The teenage boy, chewing a large wad of tobacco-infused gum, picking his nose, rolled down the driver's-side window. He gave Paul a sideways glance of notice. Music was playing.

"Pull over there! Shut her down!" Paul said with authority.

"What?" came the reply.

"Don't piss me off anymore, Sir, you heard what I said ... PARK IT! ... NOW!"

What was asked, was done. There was no more funny business. Dead silence; even the music was turned off. The usual license, insurance, registration routine then ensued. Trooper Joe was taking notes, flipping pages back as fast as he could. Paul was doing all the talking.

"What the hell were you up to? ... Didn't you see there was an accident? ... You blind or something? ... Didn't you see that fireman back there directing? ... What drug store did you buy your license at? ..... You beat all!"

The kid just sat there. Didn't budge a muscle or say a thing.

"Well? ... Say something! ... You do know how to speak, don't you? ... Obviously you don't know shit about much else. What blame excuse an idiot like you gonna try to feed me? Come on, speak up!" Paul was hot under the collar, but he was on a roll.

"What am I supposed to say?"

He must have swallowed his gum—he wasn't chewing anymore.

"Didn't you see there was an accident? Didn't you think to at least slow down? Didn't you see the person directing traffic to the other lane?" Paul gave him a long, low stare.

"The fireman? ... The guy directing traffic? ... He ain't no fucking Cop! ... He's a fireman. I don't have to do what a fuckin' fireman tells me, do I? He ain't got no authority on a highway out here, does he? ... What the fuck, man."

Paul couldn't believe what he'd just heard. That really put the icing on the cake—thick! Paul was directing Trooper Joe to write faster. The trooper flipped to the next page of his notebook. Trooper Joe would have a lot more paperwork to do before Paul was finished with the clown before him. Pages kept flipping; Paul kept his nose an inch from the guilty party's face, barking at him loudly. The boy was shrinking in the driver seat. Paul was going to be rich!

Paul had no use for idiots, very little patience with them. After five more minutes of barking, Paul finally walked away. He went fishing through his gear for his tobacco pouch. He found it, filled his pipe, kept walking.

Junior was left in the capable hands of Trooper Joe. The guilty party was now in handcuffs, seated in the back of the state police cruiser. A large dog, looking quite hungry, was seated beside him. Junior was wetting his pants for the third time, with the dog back there keeping him company. There were over two dozen violations Paul had Trooper Joe staple to the idiot child's shirt! Junior didn't get to go skiing that weekend!

Cars in the accident were towed by different tow trucks, from the scene, back to the tow company gas stations, locked up in their towing yards. Junior's sports buggy was also towed away. The impound yard, at the state police barracks, had a special area for that vehicle. It was labeled "Parking for Idiots Only" way out back!

Westland Fire & Rescue stayed until the last battered car was on its way on a flatbed. Blue Angel ambulances had taken all injured parties to hospitals long ago. Not much left of two of the vehicles. A lot of Speedy Dry was used. We cleaned up parts, pieces, a lot of glass. When all was done; cones, other implements that had been used, were shoved back into their respective spaces on engines, utility trucks, or rescue vehicles. All was under control, scene was cleared, all returning to quarters.

Greg and George were both at the station. We had a half-hour's worth of chores to finish up before all units were called back in, ready to go. Paul had come back to the station, too. He had his pipe going. All was calm. He was pondering some ATV tracks, mixed with others, in the field across from the station.

George and Greg wanted to play a few games of cribbage, asked me to find a fourth player as a partner. Caleb Mills had just finished spraying down an engine, walked into the main meeting room from the bays.

"A little cribbage, Caleb?" I asked.

"Cribbage? ...You as a partner? ... You can't play worth shit! ... No way you're getting me into a game, man. I don't have money to burn the way you clowns do!"

I think the cribbage gods spoke to him, gave him false information! We played three-way for four games. I actually won one game!

I talked with Paul the next afternoon. He'd pulled into the library parking lot, across the street from my house. There to slow the locals down for an hour or so. He'd back his cruiser into a parking space between two cars, then wait. His window was down, he was smoking the corn-cob. Mike, with his great head out the back window behind Paul, tail going a mile a minute, was happy to see me.

"AaaahRoooo."

I looked down the outside of Paul's cruiser. I think I found the true reason Paul never had to wash his car!

"Anything on the burner?" I asked.

"Not much," Paul answered. "Nice weather for a change, my State Police folk found the Lapan family finally ... Folks that bought the place on Old Oakwood Road ... They have a daughter off at a fancy boarding school someplace. Trying to make some contact with her. Make sure she's alright and all. They didn't think she'd be up at the new place, but you never know. They're working on trying to find her. On school vacation right now, you know."

Two large smoke rings slowly drifted out the window. The engine was in park, on idle. Mike liked the flavor of my right hand, for some unknown reason. Between long pats, or large ear scratches, he had decided my hand should be properly licked to death. My shirt sleeve was getting soaked. Paul was still talking.

"They should be coming up from Jersey next weekend. They want to see what there is left of the place ... figure out what to do next. Haven't heard if they want to build again, or not. Pretty much up in the air. I'd like to meet with them, though, when they get around to it."

More rings of smoke wafted out the window. Paul looked down the road to his left.

"Got one!" Paul said.

A pale blue four-door sedan came toward us. Paul clicked on his blue lights. The sedan slowed down quickly. Paul clicked the blues off: "Just a warning, Sir, keep it under if you don't mind. Thank you so much!" We were both thinking the same thing! Five minutes later, a green Beamer came screaming through.

It is a thirty-five-mile-an-hour zone through the village. Not a smidgen more than that! Fifty-five does not cut it with this constable, no Sir! It would not do at all! Constable Whipple was on him like a tick on Michelangelo. Had that fellow pulled over, in front of pretty blue lights, before he'd gone fifty feet past? "No excuses for you, Sir. Please pull out your wallet!"

CHAPTER 8

The mystery of the Lapan family's whereabouts was finally solved. They were now back in Scotch Plains, New Jersey. They returned Tuesday from a lovely two-week cruise around the Florida Keys. They did some island hopping, parasailing, snorkeling, had a wonderful time with friends. The state police had their home telephone number on file, given to them from the Lapans' neighbors. The SP gave the number to Paul, who in turn, contacted the Lapans by cell phone.

They were coming up from New Jersey on Amtrak Friday night. They would have a rental car, motel accommodations, already booked ahead, waiting for them, when arriving. Paul arranged to meet with them Saturday afternoon around three in their No Tell Motel lobby.

Paul arrived at the motel early. A thirty-unit with office, dining facility, conference room, hospitality suite, all quite clean, inviting. The Lapans were already in the lobby waiting for Officer Whipple. Mr. Lapan was a good-looking, late-forties/early-fifties gentleman, about six foot tall, slightly balding. He had a dark blue sweater over a lighter blue dress shirt, nicely tailored pressed pants, penny loafers. She was tall, long haired, sandy blonde. Dark hazel eyes, well tanned, off-white business suit with light yellow blouse, gold necklace with matching bracelet. She had an infectious smile.

"James Lapan, my wife Gail. Officer Whipple, isn't it?" He had a firm handshake.

"Paul Whipple, Sir, but just call me Paul."

Cob was in his upper vest pocket, unlit. They sat down in the small hospitality room to the left of the lobby. There was coffee, doughnuts, other assorted treats. Paul grabbed a cup, filled it two-thirds up, added half-and-half, no sugar, handed it to Mrs. Lapan. She nodded, thanked him politely. The second cup was poured exactly the same for himself. Mr. Lapan nibbled on a doughnut. They were at a small table by the window, looking down on the Connecticut River.

The Lapans explained in depth how they had been on their lovely vacation. They had no idea that there had been any fire at all. That was, until their return to New Jersey. They had listened to a long string of phone messages, backlogs of the past two weeks. There was a repeated message to please call the Vermont State Police. A number was given, please call at their earliest convenience. Paul found out from Gail Lapan that their daughter, Suzanne, had also been on vacation. No, they had not heard from her in the last three weeks.

Rockwell Fleetwood Academy, Suzanne Lapan's prep school over in New Hampshire, was presently still on vacation. It was the prep school's winter break. Everyone would be returning to campus on this next coming Monday. James as well as Gail Lapan did not know how to reach their daughter. Nor did they know where she might have gone to at the present time. Suzanne was a free spirit. A sophomore, straight-"A" student, was trusted to be on her own any time she pleased. Her parents didn't seem worried at all, not knowing where she was, or went.

Paul conversed with the Lapans for over an hour. They had many questions for Paul ... How did it start? ... What happened? ...Was anything saved? ... Who called the fire department? ... Why didn't anyone see it sooner? ... Who can we thank that responded? ... Paul answered as best he knew how. He did, however, have one last question to ask of Gail Lapan.

"Does Suzanne cook, Mrs. Lapan?" Paul asked.

"Suzanne cook? Oh Dear, NO!" Gail let out a laugh, smiled. "Mr. Whipple, Suzanne doesn't know how to boil water! I don't think I've ever seen her cook even a TV dinner! She eats properly, but, I'm afraid James loves to do all the cooking in our household. I cook on occasion. Oh! Suzanne does do popcorn in the microwave!" She laughed again. She had a nice twinkle to her eyes, with a warm smile.

"Why would you ask a silly question like that?" she puzzled.

"Oh it is nothing, really," said Paul. Nothing but a piece of his puzzle fitting together in his mind. It wasn't until Monday afternoon that Paul heard again from the Lapans. He got a jingle on his cell.

"Mr. Whipple? This is Gail Lapan.

"I just got off the phone with Roger Dow, Headmaster at Rockwell Fleetwood Academy, Suzanne's school."

There was a different tone to Gail Lapan's voice. It was more concerned sounding. She continued, "He informed me that my daughter, Suzanne, never showed for classes today. Her roommate, Julie Smith, that Mr. Dow had spoken with, had not seen her as well. Are you there, Officer Whipple?"

Paul answered, "Yes, Mrs. Lapan, please continue."

"This is very disturbing to me, Mr. Whipple." Her voice almost had a tremble.

"Our Suzanne has never missed a class since fifth grade, when she was ill. I thought you should know."

There was a slight letting out of breath in her soft-spoken voice. Paul thanked her for calling with this very important message, thanked her a second time. The call ended … Interesting, very interesting, he thought.

Four days later, Suzanne Lapan was still missing. State Police had contacted the Lapan family, asked if Suzanne had any dental records that they knew of. The Lapans thought this to be a strange request. A strange request, until the cat was let loose from the bag. They were then informed for the first time that a body had been found within the burned ruins of their farmhouse. That information had not been spread around to too many people, especially not to the press. Those few that did know were sworn to keep it under wraps by both the state police and Paul the constable. Too many noses poking around could mess up what investigation was still progressing. Both Lapans were in shock when told about it.

Mr. Lapan thought Suzanne's dentist, near Scotch Plains in New Jersey, should have any information they might need. He would contact the dental office, see if they could fax Suzanne's most recent records, including X-ray pictures, up to the address given them by the state police. The address was the forensics lab where the burnt remains of a young female had been taken. The police didn't mention that part to the Lapans.

Forensics got what they needed within the week. It didn't take the lab very long to run a few tests, compare results. It was confirmed that the remains found in the house, and the missing straight-"A" student, were one and the same. Suzanne Lapan had been located. There was no doubt the body found belonged to her.

The state police, when forensics shared their results, informed Suzanne's parents. Unbelief, shock were replaced by a breakdown of flooding tears. How could this be? Too much was happening at once. Their minds had taken the information in, had then malfunctioned on overload. They didn't want the information to be true. It can't be true! They tried in desperation to set their minds someplace else, a different time zone, a different outcome—anything but this! Oh, God! ... Oh, God! ... Not Suzanne! ... Oh, God!!

What was left of the body of Suzanne Lapan was released from the forensics lab, flown down to New Jersey to be cremated. The funeral would be a week or so later. There were plans made to have a memorial service at the Rockwell Fleetwood Academy as well. Suzanne was a popular student there. The news of her death upset many of her young, good friends.

James and Gail Lapan were back in New Jersey with relatives, friends, all trying to decompress. They had returned to Scotch Plains

via Amtrak a few days after the state police had visited. They were still both shaken, coping, trying to breathe a little better, if breathe at all.

Salty was walking with me that day when we saw their noon train go by. We were down on Spring Falls Road in Paleyville. The railroad tracks go close above the river there for a couple of miles. It's a pretty road down there all year. Foliage over the river is picturesque beauty in the fall. Geese, flying low, landing by the large "S" bend in open water. They are there most of the year. Ice flows are neat, snow-covered trees beautiful; silence in the winter cold.

That day it was sunny, with just a few small clouds floating quickly by. The ice, below us on the river's bend, had just started breaking up. You could hear large pieces rounding the large bend, not making their turn, crashing into the bank, then continuing slowly downriver. It was exciting to witness, listen to, watch.

Geese were coming back. Seven or eight would fly low over the ice flow, passing Salty with me looking on, heading upriver past the bend. There was a stretch of open water half a mile up, just beyond a small island, where they could land. A mile upstream, you could hear the honking of many as the seven that flew by us were greeted as they came, honking themselves, in for a landing.

Spring Falls Road was a good place to walk

the dog. Salty, on leash with me, would walk there almost every day during the warmer months, not so much so during the winter. Both of us loved watching the trains go by. We knew the Amtrak southbound schedule fairly well. Salty's ears would perk up five minutes before I ever heard a train whistle, or heard the distinctive rush of wind coming down the track.

Once in a while, a far-off train whistle would let us know they were close, coming our way, up afar on the edge of the river. Dogs have good ears. Every so often we would get lucky. Salty's ears would perk up. I had not heard a thing. Moments later, an unexpected freight would be going by, brightly graffiti-decorated boxcars going north or south, creaking along, two engines pulling steadily with strength to spare.

The Lapans could be reached at any time down there in New Jerseyville. It wasn't a good time now to bother them with more questions. The Lapans had too much on their plates. Time to let the dust settle a bit, try to find a lost smile, reflect, remember, pray.

Paul was at the firehouse with us. Not much going on. The trucks were all tucked away with the doors down. Inside, four of us were playing doubles at the long table in the main meeting room. Paul was seated at the far end of the table, elbows on the table, smoking his pipe. Mike was flopped down at his feet, intently watching a small black beetle going across the linoleum. Paul had something on his mind. You could see the wheels turning.

"Department has that big ATV still, doesn't it?" he asked, hand on his chin, holding the cob pipe.

"Sure. It's out in the back of bay two. Guys had it out yesterday running around the field with it. Wanted to see how well she's running, and all. Fueled her up again, checked everything. Why you asking?" J.J. replied.

"Mind if I look her over?" Paul asked.

"Not at all. Have at it. You'll see it back there. Why? What's up?" George was the one that answered, now curious himself. He was munching on a cookie, bag full on the table near him.

"Oh, just curious," came Paul's reply.

Paul got up, walked in no particular hurry toward the door to the bays. We continued playing cribbage.

"Count your stupid hand, dummy!" I said.

"Sixteen!" came the reply.

George could pull the right card out of the deck every time. How he does it, we'll never know!

Paul inched around the tanker, found the ATV set back next to a stack of sandbags. Bay two, right where they said it was. All balloon tires looked brand new. Bigger, wider tread than what he was looking for. Not a scratch or gouge in any of them. Paul let out a "humph." No luck here. He went back to the card players.

"Who else owns ATVs around here?" Smoke ring rising.

"Hell, I think half the young guys here have one; a few over-the-hill buzzards have 'em as well. You come by on a Sunday morning, when we're working on stuff, there will be a dozen or so out there," J.J. said.

"Humph!" came Paul's reply.

Sunday morning came. Paul pulled up to the station, parked in the mud. There were pick-ups plus a few cars there ahead of him. All were all neatly parked at forty-five-degree angles across from the bay doors, on the other side of Fireman's Trail. In the field behind the pickups were seven ATVs, plus three snowmobiles with their engines on idle. No one was in sight, all inside the station. Two of the snowmobiles were brand-new Polaris beauties. Twin dark blues with yellow lightning bolts down each side. Very snazzy! The third was an older model, all electric green in color. Had a few dings and scratches.

Paul didn't notice any of the three snow machines. He had his hand on his chin, pipe in hand. He went right by the snow machines, tunnel-visioned, over to the string of ATVs. He slowly walked the line of them, inspecting each as he went.

He found what he was looking for. The third

ATV in line, parked a foot in front of the others. It was a dark green monster, maybe four or five years old. It had a good gouge of rubber out of the right front wheel. It looked like it had been there a while. Paul was hunched down, lighting his pipe, observing the wheel, when a snowball lobbed past him, buried itself in the snow. It missed his head by a good foot. Paul let out a couple of puffs, looked up to see where the projectile had come from.

CHAPTER 9

"Whatcha looking at?"

It was Caleb Mills. He had just come out of the firehouse, dressed in quilted, zipper-legged, suspender ski pants. Had on boots, gloves, open jacket, knit hat. He saw Paul hunched down, looking at the front of his machine. Caleb decided to make himself a snowball, see if Mr. Constable was awake! Paul hadn't noticed him. That was when the snowball lobbed past.

"Just looking" was Paul's reply.

"Wheel here, has a good chunk out of it. This buggy yours?"

Caleb smiled.

"Yeah, sure is. I bought her secondhand last year. Tire came that way. Don't hurt it none. That tire's lasted pretty good. She runs like a top, most of the time. Old fart like you'd most likely fall off!"

He was chewing the last of a Snickers bar.

"They got coffee going inside. Welcome to some if you want."

His jaw was getting a workout from the cara-
mel, peanuts, chocolate conglomeration slowly
going down his throat. Paul blew smoke in his
face as he walked by, heading toward the station, some coffee, doughnuts, and possibly some
good morning chatter.

Greg was sitting at the dispatch desk. George,
beside me, was sitting on the edge of a large
equipment box a freight company had delivered.
We were in the dispatch room, chewing, chattering, drinking coffee. Paul joined us with a cup of
his own, a doughnut with one bite taken out.

"That kid out there ... member of the
department?"

Paul played with his lips, blew a huge smoke
ring toward the ceiling.

"Caleb? He's been around a couple of years.
Got interested when he was in high school.
Mouthy little bastard at times, but he's a hard
worker. Does what he's told at a fire. Not a bad
guy really," Greg said, drumming the eraser of
his pencil on the tabletop.

We all finished off what doughnuts were
left, had a few cups of coffee more. We were still
chattering away about nothing in particular.
A good twenty minutes went by. We heard the
front door open, then slam shut, behind someone. Moments later, Caleb Mills was standing in
the dispatch doorway. Hands fumbling around
in his jacket pocket.

"You old geezers haven't left yet. I thought it'd be past your bedtimes by now," he said.

"Can you come over, sit on the bed, tuck me in, read us a bedtime story, give me a big kiss good night?!" George said with a grin.

"Go fuck yourself, Kratch Muffin. You can kiss my ass!"

We all chuckled at Caleb. He pulled another Snickers out of his jacket.

"Rot your teeth, you eat enough of those," taunted Paul with a smile.

Caleb said he was about to take off, back to the West-West, before the sun went down. He didn't mind riding in the dark, had a good headlight, but it was easier riding in the daylight.

Greg said he was about ready to lock up, head on out, as well. Four paper coffee cups took aim at the basket. Ready, aim, shoot! Three three-pointers went in. Mine, of course, bounced off the rim, and out. I sank the rebound—all net! One last check around the dispatch desk; all in order, we locked the office door behind us.

We all ambled out toward the front door. Greg locked the front door behind us as the last one passed through. He pushed multiple numbers on the lock keypad under the doorknob. We all then fanned out toward the parking lot. One by one, our cars, pickups, or duct-taped ancient antiques, with wheels attached, filed down Fireman's Trail. Some to go south, north, or straight across toward the west. Caleb was across the field, quickly out of sight in a flash, heading toward the West-West trail.

We had three calls on Tuesday—nothing very major. First call was at Richard Dobbs'. Richard is one of our "frequent fliers." The fire was out back, same usual place, same station. He would set it behind his double-wide, forty-year-old, pink with blue prefabricated abode. The house was slowly falling in from disrepair. Third fire call we had there in the past month. Dicky would build up a bonfire out of any illegal burnables he'd dig up on the property. There was plenty of stuff to choose from. He had junk piles every place you looked. There were large lumps here, there, all about the place. Looked something like moguls on a ski slope, when they were snow covered.

Sometimes just a small burn pile, sometimes way too big. The fires Dicky set always had a good, thick jet-black smoke column going up. Very easy to see from a distance. You first got a whiff of the nasty-smelling stench coming up long before actually seeing fire. We don't know what he used to start his infernos with. Whatever it was, the bonfire would be roaring by the time we were called.

We would respond, yank a hose line off an engine, put it out. It was a good practice drill for "rookies"! Chief would go over, chew Dicky out.

Tell him never to light a match in Westland ever again. Paul would level a good-sized fine every time. Then away we would go. "Dicky Dobber" was deaf as a post. He never listened. The town, or Paul, never got rich off him. "Dobber" didn't have five cents to his name. Most likely used the citations to start the next fire.

Dicky Dobber, alias Richard Dobbs—maybe the other way around—was now in his forties. He got his nickname in high school. During his junior year, he was going with Stephanie ... Stephanie Whatzserbod. They were an inseparable couple. Glue was stuck real good with those two. They were together since his freshman year. Trouble was she got pregnant. Big stink made about it. Her parents were old-school Romans. They didn't approve of consensual, consequential sex. Her baby was put up for adoption as soon as it was born. Steph, whole family, moved someplace down south after that.

That's when Richard got the nickname. Once nickname glue is applied, nicknames stick forever. Maybe it was a good thing. Dobber never amounted to much after he graduated from high school. A lot of folks thought he never really got over what happened. Very sad—tragic really. Fire department thinks he should have been nicknamed "*Marvin the Torch*" instead of Dicky Dob. Oh well, life goes on.

The third call Tuesday was sprinkled with sweet-and-sour sauce. A call down near the Paleyville line, on the Cow Path Road. Miss Beaumont, an eighty-seven-year-old widow living alone. It was a medical alarm call. The problem was unknown. The alarm company couldn't reach her to confirm a problem existed—her line was always busy.

We took off with the tone. Blue Angel was close behind. When we arrived at Miss Beaumont's small cottage, we found her sitting primly on her living-room couch talking with her next-door neighbor. She explained in depth that she was perfectly fine, there was no problem at all. She had no idea why the alarm system had malfunctioned. Miss Beaumont was a very proper lady. Her mind was still sharp as a tack most of the time. She had outlived two husbands, went back to her maiden name of Beaumont. She preferred Miss over Mrs., Ma'am, or Madam. Only a few close friends she'd known for thirty years or more dared call her Ann, or Annie.

C-1, the Chief, went into her bedroom to reset the alarm system. The system was on the nightstand, next to her properly made bed, with hand-stitched quilt at the foot. C-1 found the telephone knocked over on the floor. Picking it up, it still had a good dial tone, buzzing at him. He called the alarm company, told

them everything was under control, he was re-
setting the system. The phone was hung up.

C-1 pushed a series of keys on the alarm system box. An orange signal light started blinking
on the top, signaling the system was up, running, reset correctly. C-1 then came out of the
bedroom, joined the rest of the throng in the living room.

Thirty seconds later, the medical alarm went
off again. The Chief went back to the bedroom to
investigate the problem. He let out a good laugh
from the bedroom door.

"Hey, guys! ... Commeer!"

Seven heads peered into the bedroom, bodies all squished into the small doorway. There,
on her bed, in total concentration, were three
of her seven cats. They were all looking intently
at the reset light on the black metal box. Every
time the machine blinked orange, indicating it
was on, running correctly, a minimum of three
paws would take a swipe at the orange blinking toy. Another cat's back would hunker down,
tail straight up, ready to pounce. Once the right
button was pressed down by a paw, the medical alarm would be activated, the orange toy
would stop blinking. A medical dispatch company automatically was called, or toned, as the
case might be. To the cats, a victory had been
achieved!

"I'm pretty sure I've found our problem,

Miss Beaumont," C-1 said, still laughing. "Your cats!"

A path was cleared so Miss Beaumont, cane in hand, could shuffle-step along to her bedroom door. She reached into her large sweater pocket for her glasses.

"Oh you naughty kitties!" she exclaimed. "Shew! ... Shew!"

Two of the cats obeyed—momentarily. They were back a minute later. C-1 unplugged the alarm system monitor only after calling the medical-alert company a second time to say what he was doing. He relocated the blinking device. Put it up on high ground in the room, hopefully out of range of her menagerie of Lions and Tigers. Miss Beaumont had a triggering device as a necklace she wore always. To put the alarm box high would not cause a problem if she needed help.

"Better leave your children out of the bedroom, Miss Beaumont," the Chief said, still chuckling.

"Oh, I will. I surely will. Thank you all so much for looking in on me. Oh, those terrible, terrible cats! They are such a bother, but I do love them all dearly."

She was sitting in her high-backed rocker; a calico, long-haired friend was purring in her lap. I was picking up our jump kit in the living room, when I actually looked at the small living room, closely, for the first time. All low-painted wood—around three doors, around all low windowsills, the low borders to all walls—wood and plaster were clawed deeply right through.

There were three places where the patterned blue wallpaper had been removed by claws dug into the plaster walls or wood framing. From the floor, three feet up all sides, the cats had destroyed all four walls of the living room. Someone needed to buy the poor lady a cat scratching post. Then again, maybe four, or five, scratching posts were needed. It was a sad sight.

CHAPTER 10

We had finished a good breakfast at Paley's.
It was a bright sunny morning. Paul
asked if I wanted to go out to Old Oakwood,
snoop around with him for a few minutes. We
stood up from the table, walked to the counter
to pay our bills. Salty had nothing earth-shatter-
ing to do so we decided to follow the constable's
cruiser, with the whip antenna, to the West.
Michelangelo had his head out the back window,
had his ears flapping in the breeze, as our cara-
van of two went along. Salty, with me driving,
stayed well back. Salty's head was out the window, too. It wasn't raining out, that Salty knew
of. We both didn't want it to pour drool if we followed too close! Paul pulled off onto what was a
very muddy Old Oakwood Road. He turned into
the freshly snow-covered drive of what used to
be the Porterson, now turned Lapan, residence.
We turned in a good distance behind. Salty excited, wanting to get out, play in the field.

You could see pieces and parts of burnt
wood, metal furniture frames, twisted pipes, the

tilted stove peeking up. There were a few places left where you could make out the remains of a wall. There were places a pipe would stand tall, reaching up at an angle to a second floor that now didn't exist. All had a snow covering, with footprints scattered about. The burnt floor had many new footprints. Not much to see of what earlier had been an 1890s stick-framed, well-maintained farmhouse.

Paul got out of the vehicle. Salty bounded out of our car, after me, as soon as I opened the driver's-side door. Mike had to slowly pour himself off the back seat of Paul's cruiser, sniff the air, walk away from the car a few feet, then sat on his back haunches.

"What now, Boss?" was written on his face. Salty was quite a bit different. After bounding over me to get out of the car, he was now running circles out in the field.

Paul, with me behind, aimed for the burned-out mass beside the driveway. Salty dog wanted to play. He turned into *"Scooter Dog,"* hunching his back end down, now running circles around Michelangelo. The Lab would be jumping around, then hunching his front down, inches away from his playmate, stop and bark. His tail would be wagging madly, then he would dash around Michelangelo in racing circles again. Very annoying!

Mike would have nothing to do with him.

There was work to be done. This golden Labrador was being a childish pain in the butt! The bloodhound looked toward the big field next to the drive. With his nose to the ground, he started out into the field going down a recently made snowmobile track. Salty took off ahead of him, luxuriating in his ability to run around free without a leash. Mike took no notice of him. He was at work. Lots of smells to ponder. To Michelangelo, the hunt was on!

Paul followed a fresh set of boot tracks into the charred remains. I followed behind, being careful where I stepped. His pipe was lit. He was poking around with a long stick he had found. The constable stopped suddenly. He was over near the stove, hand on his chin.

"Now that's different," he said. "Come here, take a look at this, will you?"

I stepped carefully over an exposed piece of pipe, stood next to him, next to the stove. I was looking where Paul was looking. I saw an ash-covered, snow-covered stove.

"What am I looking at?" I queried.

"Knobs," said Paul. "Two missing."

I looked again. He was right. Two burnt metal knobs, that had controlled the larger burners on the stovetop, were missing. Someone had taken a knife, or pry bar of sorts, to very roughly pull each one of them off the front. Many small scratch marks were left behind.

"Seems a little strange to me. Seem strange to you?"

His pipe had a pretty good head of steam. Paul was adding more puzzle pieces to the heap he had sorted neatly in his mind. Lots of puzzle pieces floating about still. We both kept digging about in the wreckage a while longer.

Mike was way out in the field where a few ATV tracks and the snowmobile track he had followed converged, making a major junction in the snow covering. Salty was still trying to dance around Mike. The Lab had found a big fallen tree limb. He was now prancing, as a horse in a horse show, his prize trophy hanging out both corners of his mouth. Mike couldn't be bothered. He had his nose in the snow. He was determined not to get annoyed.

"AhhaaaaaRoooo."

Mike was on to something. It took Paul, with me out of breath, trudging behind on the trail a good fifteen minutes to make it across to where the two dogs were. Mike hadn't moved from his position. The two of us avoided the soft wet spots scattered about as much as we could. A few cows had been out there, left good-sized piles of calling cards, snow covered but noticeable.

Mike still had his nose down. He hadn't dug at all, had found something close to the surface. When we got to him, Paul pulled his collar back, took a look where Mike's nose had been a second earlier. Something caught Paul's eye.

He took a large mitten off his hand, brushed lightly with it over the snow covering. There in the snow, half buried, very shiny, were four spent .22 casings. They looked fairly new compared to the others Mike had found for him.

Out popped a plastic sandwich bag. Paul always came prepared. He placed the shells inside, zip-locked it tight, stuffed it in his pocket. A smoke ring drifted slowly, grew bigger, then melted away down the field in the morning breeze.

"Interesting," he said.

We started back toward the cars. Mike followed, nose still to the ground. Mike hopped into Paul's cruiser when they got there. Paul was in front, Mike in back. Paul gave us a wave, and both went on their way back to the East.

It took a little longer to convince Salty we were leaving. He had no intention of leaving his new home on the range. No dog leaves without first thoroughly killing the small tree proudly hanging from his mouth. The silly dog had work he intended to do. Each limb of his monster branch had to be inspected, branches methodically chewed off the main stem, then shredded to fine mulch. Next, this mulch had to be spread on the field very evenly.

The dog's intention was to cover this whole

three-acre field with chewed mulch. It would be as a cover before spring seed planting. It was a very thoughtful, neighborly task to do, Salty thought. It was his duty as a dog to do it! He had no intention of leaving! Leave! ... Leave! ... You expect me to leave when I'm having this much fun! ... Oops! ... Work! ... I mean work!

The next limb, which was destined for the same fate as the previously chewed limb, was now slowly being devoured. It was a good twenty minutes later before his muddy paws bounded across the front seat to the passenger side of the RAV-4.

No, I wasn't going to chase him all around the field all that time. Oh! He would have loved that! He did have a good time of it, out there on the range. He had a bad habit of leaving me a full-bodied mud-pie cushion to sit upon whenever the opportunity arose. When he bounded into the car, going across my side to his portion of the front seats, he would do it. Dripping globs of mud were left just for me, all over my seat! I know he thought it was funny! Horses have horse smiles. Dogs can have dog smiles. Salty had a big dog smile! We headed east for home. The roads were wet from runoff, but most of the ice was gone. Salty was curled asleep, tired from all his hard work out in the field.

I was the next one that fell asleep. That evening, I dozed off watching the game show

Wheel. It was early. Salty joined me as we went to bed hours before our scheduled time to go up to the Land of Nod. I awoke late as well. Salt was already up. He had finished his breakfast, came back upstairs to see if I was up. My feet had made it halfway to the cold floor.

Salty's front paws were up on the bed. My left hand getting a vigorous lick-down. He was indicating it was past the regular morning "*tummy rub*" time. There wasn't enough room for him to bound up onto the bed, small bedroom. I knew he could get up there easily on his own if he really wanted to do it. We had a morning ritual to follow, however. He thought it important that I help him up, hoist his back end onto the four-poster every single morning. It was tradition!

Once up, he would roll onto his back in his customary praying position. A good tummy rub for a minimum of five minutes was then expected. I, in turn, would get many licks of appreciation. Salty was one of the few dogs that also liked sleeping on his back. Front paws up, the praying position, back legs splayed out for the world to see. Head would be to one side with his tongue out. He would be snoring softly within minutes. Oh! ... Did I forget to mention he liked to hog the whole bed at night, too? I'd get one corner with a little leftover blanket, if I was lucky!

The next time I saw Paul was a week later. He came by the station. I had just finished spray-washing, soaping up, scrubbing, spraying again my RAV-4. The station had a good power washer, hose line. The car looked a lot better—not great, just better. Still needed a few more spots to be worked on. Salty was watching from the back seat.

It was Sunday morning. He pulled up beside me, rolled down the window, let all the smoke drift out, nodded a good morning. He looked down the usual row of snowmobiles, RVs parked across the road. He looked them over a second time, didn't see what he was looking for. Mike was in the back seat, tail wagging. The Congregational church bells started tolling out the time, chimed out two songs.

"Caleb coming 'round that you know of?" he asked, not seeing Caleb's buggy in the snow.

Caleb came around almost every Sunday morning—for a while anyway. I hadn't seen him yet that Sunday.

"Should be, I expect. Haven't seen him yet," I answered. "Want me to give that thing you drive a good scrub behind the ears?"

Paul shut the cruiser down, rolled up his windows, headed into the station for coffee. He might listen to the regular muckie-muck gossip of the day some firemen had to share. He left the cruiser, Mike in the back, in my capable hands to be made spotless by the time he returned.

I scrubbed it up the best I could. Soap bubbles

all over the place. They were running down the sides as I scrubbed. They would be dripping to the ground, meandering slowly toward the drain. I got most of the major mud, goop, dog slime off it, then hosed it all down again, giving it a final rinse.

I was just starting to wind the power hose back onto its reel when I heard an ATV rounding the far corner of the field. It was Caleb Mills. I saw him, he saw me. He ran that monster of his right between two parked ATVs, through a few mud puddles, across Fireman's Trail. He pulled a three-sixty right beside me, inches away. Mud went flying! Two more complete tight circles were made. Then he came to a stop.

I was soaked. This half side of Paul's cruiser was mud dripping down, all large and small globs of it! Mike was not impressed in the back seat, either! Caleb raised the shield on his helmet face.

"Hey, *Road Cone*!" he said. "Didn't see you there, standing all alone. You could have been hit! Should have had a few cones out!"

"*Dumb Bastard*" were the first two words that flashed into my mind. I opened the power hose up full blast, attempting to spray him down in good shape. Caleb got a little wet, but he was fast on that thing. He accelerated, made a speedy escape, quickly out of range. He stayed mostly dry, darn it!

Paul came out of an open bay, smoke drifting slowly.

"Thought you said you were going to clean that thing," he said, looking toward his car. I could see he was laughing at me on the inside. I started all over again with the bubbles, brush, sprayer.

When Caleb parked, shut the ATV down, Paul walked over to him.

"Hi, Caleb, got a minute?" he asked.

"No problem, Mr. Whipple. What's up?" Caleb answered.

Having re-bubbled, scrubbed, and sprayed Paul's car again, the three of us then walked through an open bay, through the door, into the main conference room. Coffeepot was perking away, making a fresh pot just for us. There were two fresh boxes of assorted doughnuts to munch. Plain, sugar, pink with sprigglies on top, jelly, cream filled, chocolate—the works were all there. They were just begging us to come on over, try one or two. We waited for the coffee, grabbed a doughnut or more, sat ourselves down at a conference room table.

"Got a couple of questions for you if you don't mind, Caleb," Paul started. "You been out to Old Oakwood Road, where the fire was, lately?"

Caleb wrinkled his brow slightly. "Sure I have. Was out there just yesterday, tooling around the field. I took a few trails out of there. Why?"

Paul asked another. "You go in the house at all? … Take anything from what was left?"

Caleb was the one that now had a worried, puzzled look on his face. "Nothing there to take, whole place is flattened. What's this all about?"

Caleb listened as Paul explained how the two turn-on knobs had been removed from the stove. Caleb wrinkled his brow again.

"I love playing with knobs, Mr. Whipple, but not the kinds on a stove, if you catch my drift. Who the hell would want burnt stove knobs?"

"You own a .22, Caleb?" Paul asked.

"Peashooter? … I got a good deer rifle. What would I want a peashooter for? … Hell no! … I don't got no .22," Caleb answered. He took out a Milky Way bar from his pull-over front pouch.

"You ask some weird questions, Officer. What you up to, anyway?"

He took a big bite of the candy bar, started chewing. Paul sort of raised his eyebrows a bit, shrugged his shoulders, walked toward the middle front door. His hand on his chin, holding the cob, blowing smoke.

"Humph! … Thanks for the info, Caleb." Paul didn't say anything else. He left the building, got in the cruiser, left with his dog. No more explanation given.

"What the hell was that all about?" Caleb asked. I told him I hadn't a clue. I then asked a stupid question on my part. I asked if he wanted to join in some cribbage with the others. I got what usually came to me for an answer.

"Fuck No!"

Caleb stayed around for another twenty minutes or so. He took Salty for a run around the field, across from the station, for me. Caleb loved Salty. Caleb had a younger brother who had all kinds of bad allergies. Pet hair sometimes made the boy get the sneezes so bad, he couldn't stop. His face would get puffed up, teary eyed, red faced. Medications to take were plentiful, helped some, but not all the time. It was quite clear there would not be a dog, or any other animal, as a pet in that household.

Caleb headed home to the West, spraying up a good rooster tail as he went. I wondered if he had petted Salty for a brotherly love reason. I bet his little brother couldn't, wouldn't, stay too close to him when he got home. Caleb had a lot of dog hair on him when he left the station.

George said he'd play a game or two of crib against me. Greg was there, but had business to attend to, had to leave for a meeting someplace. George got out the board, we played. Salty lay down under the table. George, lucky little bastard, was a goodly wide margin ahead of me. He was on home street, I wasn't, playing the second game.

He needed twenty points to go out, win the game. I needed seven holes to peg, to just get over the skunk line. Skunks counted as two games against you, instead of just one. If you were less than thirty-one holes behind, it was only one game lost. It was just one, one game lost—not two! I was more than thirty-one holes behind. If I didn't make it over the line, George had me.

I pegged three points of the seven needed, leaving me four short of being over the skunk line. George pegged only one, leaving him nineteen holes to go. Momentarily, I felt I was safe. I had an eight-point hand still left to count. I was the one that dealt the hands out, however. I had the crib as an extra hand. By rule, George got to count his hand first before I could count hand, plus crib.

"*Lucky Boy*" laid his cards face up on the table. Two sevens, two eights, the cut card was a six. George shook his head from one side to the other.

"Damn! ... Sixteen! ... I thought I had you beat," he exclaimed.

He was about to peg the sixteen points, when I stopped him. It was I now shaking my head.

"Count it again, dummy! ... It's twenty-four!"

"Oh, yeah! I counted it wrong! Sorry. I guess you're skunked!" He pegged out.

I don't know how George does it! He pulls the right card out of his butt every time! He doesn't even know how to count the damn hand when he does it! I went home after losing two more games to him. Stupid game! Weather called for snow flurries. I wasn't happy about anything: cards, weather, luck I never had! Bah! Humbug! I went out to the car with Salty. I gave Salty a hug, got a lick or two in return. That puppy always made me feel better about life in general.

CHAPTER 11

Paul had a small, comfortable office in the town hall. Wasn't big by any means. Stained, abused old wood floor, desk with a high-backed black leather cushioned chair behind. To the side wall, three tall gray filing cabinets with a lot of papers stacked on top, a few more sticking out of drawers. Three very old, all oak, ladder-backed chairs were scattered in front of his desk, in no particular order. There was a small table with a coffeepot, burner plate plugged into the wall, three ceramic mugs. The condiments were hidden away out of sight. A large curtain half-shaded a window behind Paul's chair. Window let in more than enough light to fill the room. Oddly enough, no smell of tobacco in the room at all. Public building had rules to follow. **No Smoking** in public buildings. Paul often mentioned the fact he'd made a mistake when he agreed with the Select Board to have his office there.

It was close to noon on Wednesday when Paul's office telephone gave him three short rings. Julia, in the main office, receives all incoming calls to the town hall. She then dispatches them out in several directions to clerks, managers, selectmen, lister folk, secretaries, or possibly the dog catcher! The constable was on her list as well. Each one had their own special combination of ring tones. Paul didn't get calls on a regular basis, so he had to think for a second before picking up the line. He answered, "Hello ..."

"Officer Whipple? ... This is Caleb ... Caleb Mills ... ," came the voice from afar.

"Yes, Caleb. I talked with you at the fire station," Paul said.

"I think I may have something for you. Maybe I do, maybe I don't. Anyway, I got to thinking about all those questions you asked me on Sunday ... about having a .22 and all."

"OK," Paul returned, fumbling for his cob, remembering where he was, letting out a low "Humph."

"What?" asked Caleb.

"Nothing, nothing. Go on," said Paul.

"I was thinking. There is this kid over here, about a mile from me, but maybe a half mile from the start of Old Oakwood Road, down where the fire was."

"Go on ... ," said Paul.

"Well, this kid, Jimmy I think his name is ... he's around thirteen, maybe fifteen years old.

He don't have Down syndrome, or anything like that, but all his marbles aren't quite in the marble bag, if you know what I mean. Maybe he was dropped on his head as a baby, or something. Anyway, Jimmy is a little slow in the noggin for a kid his age ..."

"OK," said Paul.

"Yeah, well, I know Jimmy has a peashooter ..... .22 .... not too careful with it, either. He thinks of himself as a big game hunter. Goes hunting through the fields all the time. Shoots at anything that moves. Hunts around his own house—around his family's property mostly. Crazy little bastard. He shoots at everything," Caleb said, then went on.

"Jimmy shot the neighbor's cat last year. That lady was some pissed off, I'll tell you! Was going to sue his family—up one side, down the other. Don't know how they really settled the mess. I guess when she actually met Jimmy, realized he had a problem upstairs, she had a soft spot for him. Forgave the kid, I don't know. I'm just guessing. I've seen him in the field out on Old Oakwood, though. He's been there a couple of times since the fire," he continued.

"Even with that peashooter of his, I give him a wide berth. I stay away from him. For all I know, he'd take me for a squirrel, blow holes all through me! Don't know if this is a help to you, or not. I was just thinking, that's all. Thought I'd let you know what I thought." Caleb was chewing something.

"Humph! ... Thanks for sharing with me, Caleb. Don't know if there's anything to it or not, but it takes a looking at. Thanks!" Both ends hung up. Paul sat back in his chair.

Immediately three short rings again came over the line. Paul answered it. The voice was a familiar one, but a little slower, more nasal, a lot lower sounding than usual. Paul sat forward in his chair, elbows on the table.

"Ah, yes. Is this Officer Whipple ... Constable Whipple, of Westland? This is the Vermont State Tax Office calling. We have records here showing your current, as well as your past, returns have been erroneous for the last thirteen years. We have evidence you owe the State just over seventy thousand dollars in overdue, back taxes. We have been trying to reach you, Mr. Whipple, for quite some time. This is a grave error on your part, Mr. Whipple. Should this matter not be resolved by this Friday, we will have to come down, arrest you, put you in jail. This is a very, very serious matter that ..."

Paul cut the caller short.

"Enough of the bullshit, *Road Cone*. You keep this baloney up, I'll be the one putting you behind the bars ... besides, I only owe them a few thousand! ... What you doing for breakfast tomorrow? ... OK, see you there. Oh! ... you stay off the phone!" Paul hung up.

Paley's was full up when we got there. Seemed like we parked a mile down. We had a twenty-minute walk to get in the door of the place. Even had a ten-minute wait for a booth to clear out, when we did get inside. Molly, one of the newer waitresses, cleared the table off, threw down a couple of green paper place mats, silverware, asked if we wanted our usual grub.

"Yes! No menus necessary," came our answer.

Coffee was brought over in two large mugs. Shortly after, a cup filled with half-and-half creamers was set before us. It was going to be a while for the burnt hash, eggs, pancakes with syrup got served to us. We had twenty or more orders ahead of us.

"Done skillfully, tastefully ... artistic, I got it," Betty said.

"A bar-shaped hard cookie made with almonds."

She was sitting at the counter, pencil in hand, newspaper in front.

"Biscotti," Paul answered.

"Right! Thank you. The belief that good will prevail over evil."

"Optimism!" They both had it at the same time. Score still tied!

"I'm going out to Old Oakwood again. Do a

little snooping with Mike," Paul said, holding his mug high enough so Molly knew he needed a refill.

"You want to tag along?" His coffee cup was being filled.

"Not today. Salty has me running some errands off. My wife gave him a good-sized list! Should take half the morning, They've been put off way too long. We need to get them done, before my queen bee kicks the two of us out of the hive. I've been pretty close to it, a few times! Don't want to get her mad at us. You take Mike, have a good time!" I said.

With my breakfast finished, Salty, who had been waiting patiently in the front seat, was then well satisfied with a belly full of bacon, Paul went west, the RAV-4, with Salty and I aboard, went north. I let Salty drive most the way home—after he finished his bacon!

Paul parked in his usual spot in the drive off Old Oakwood Road. He put a long leash on Mike; they both started walking out into the field. Mike found several more shell casings, an old tomato soup can, too. The two of them had been snooping through the snow for about half an hour when Paul first noticed a figure, standing silently, at the corner of the field. He had a bright red jacket, dungarees, boots, hunting cap with ear flaps. Oh, he also had a .22-caliber rifle under his arm!

He stood by a small stand of birch trees about fifty yards away. Paul, Mike on leash, walked toward him. He had not moved, but then waved his hand. He had a smile on his face.

"Hi," Paul said. "You must be Jimmy."

"Yup! ... I'm Jimmy Wallace. I'm a hunter. You're a fireman. I can tell a fireman. You have a badge!" observed Jimmy.

"Do you hunt here much, Jimmy?" asked Paul.

"Yup. I like to hunt a lot. I'm a good hunter. Hunters provide food for their families. Did you know that? Are you a hunter?" Jimmy answered.

"Did you know the lady that lived here?" Paul questioned, digging out his tobacco pouch.

"She's naughty ... She doesn't like me to hunt ... She didn't like hunters ... She yelled at me ... I don't like her ... She's a naughty lady." Jimmy had a frown on his face.

"Have you been over to the house that burned here, Jimmy?" A match was lit, tobacco started burning.

"Yup," he answered.

"Did you ever take anything out of the burned house, Jimmy?" Paul was going fishing at this point.

Jimmy stepped back, giving Paul a hard look.

"I found them first! ... They're mine! ... I got souvenirs! ... You can't have them! ... You're naughty, I don't like you anymore!" Jimmy looked frightened.

Paul took in a puff of smoke.

"Oh, you can keep the souvenirs, Jimmy, I don't want them. The ones you took from the front of the stove, right?"

"They're mine!" said Jimmy. "I still think you're naughty! ... I'm going home! ... I'm going home right now! ... I don't want to talk to you! ... You're a naughty man!"

Jimmy turned himself around quickly. He ran past the stand of snow-covered birch, then headed down a small trail into the deeper woods, out of sight, silently as a deer.

"Humph." Paul blew a smoke ring. Strange little kid, but interesting, he thought to himself. He turned Mike around, large head pointed in the right direction, both headed back toward the driveway. Paul's mind was at work. He had puzzle pieces laid out. He thought a few of them might be coming together.

CHAPTER 12

Two days later, Paul was behind his desk at his town hall office. His feet were up, hands were down, glasses low on his nose. In low-mode concentration, he was finishing the final fold of a newly designed paper airplane. This model was about to be given its maiden flight from his desktop across to a round circular landing zone near the coffeepot. The landing zone had a few used paper cups, soiled napkins, stir-sticks in its hangar—plenty of room left for an aircraft.

Green uniformed with a "Smokey the Bear" on top, State Trooper Joseph Tidmore, alias Trooper Joe, knocked, politely entered the room. Feet came down from the desktop. Paul straightened up, fumbled with a few papers on his desk, the late-model aircraft hidden beneath.

Trooper Joe had some paperwork from a previous two-vehicle altercation call both he, alongside Paul, had attended. Two duplicate documents that needed Paul's signatures on pages three, nine, eleven, also fifteen, for the state police records. Joe placed the papers on Paul's desk, closed the office door behind him. He explained what was needed where. He showed Paul the exact lines that needed to be signed, then dated. Paul was offered a pen, started flipping pages. John Hancocks were being scribbled on the lines where Trooper Joe was pointing, dates witnessed by Joe.

Joe Tidmore was just being the messenger boy today. It didn't hurt that he knew there would be coffee brewing, hopefully a few doughnuts available. Joe knew Paul's small office with the big window quite well. All police, most firemen liked a good doughnut with a fresh cup of coffee to wash it down with. Good stuff! Most police knew every spot in town to find both. They had good noses!

Paul was just about finished with the second signature, second copy, when his office door burst open. A short man in muck boots, old jeans, stained work shirt, a red-green all-checkered hunting jacket stormed in. It was obvious he was steamed up about something. He had Jimmy Wallace, by an ear, in tow. Jimmy, on tiptoe, hop-skipped into the room, looking scared to death.

"This the man you was talking with, Son?" he yelled at the boy.

"Yup," came the reply.

Jimmy was bent down, looking at the floor. Jimmy's father was the football player type.

Broad-shouldered, barrel-chested, husky-mus-
cular bloke. Looked strong as an ox. Paul could
see this bull was a little angry. The grand entrance just made, added to the tone of his voice,
made it easy to detect!

"You! ... You're the goddamn sheriff here in
this town, ain't cha! ... What the hell you been
talking to my boy, Jimmy, about? ... I don't want
Jimmy talking to you, or anybody else, without
my permission! Got it?! ... I'll sue your dumb
ass! My lawyer wasn't present, was he? ... No he
weren't! ... My Jimmy, here, is just a minor. You
can't use what he says ... You understand that?
... Got it?!" Mr. Wallace was already red in the
face.

"Absolutely," said Paul, chair tilted back.
Paul was about to put his feet up again, but ow-
ing to the present situation, thought better of it
at the last minute. His chair tilted upright again.
Paul wished he could blow smoke in the man's
face, but the pipe rule was in effect. Rats!

"Sit on down, Mr. Wallace, for a minute. Like
some coffee? Made it fresh," Paul asked in a very
calm voice.

"No, I don't want yer damn coffee," he
answered.

The man did sit down, however, on one of the
ladderbacks in front of Paul's desk. It was sur-
prising the lacquer on Mr. Wallace's chair didn't
start peeling from all the steam being applied to

it. Officer Whipple was amused. Jimmy stood at attention next to his father, his head still bent down looking through the floorboards. A shiver ran through his body. He tried not to move a muscle as his father's voice raged on. Trooper Joe was by the filing cabinets, a mug of coffee in hand, the now closed office door to his left. He was listening with one eye cocked toward Paul.

"You ever been out on Old Oakwood Road where the farmhouse burned recently, Mr. Wallace?" Paul asked, again very calmly. Mr. Wallace looked up with a furrowed brow. He put his two large hands on his knees, elbows bent, body forward, hard staring at Paul.

"What the hell you want to know that for? Yes, I've been over there a couple of times, looking around, hunting with my boy. Why?" came the wary answer, still staring without a blink. The man's expression had changed slightly. He now looked worried for some unknown reason.

"You know the family that recently bought the place. Ever meet any of them?" asked Paul.

"No. Never," came the father's sharp, quick answer.

Jimmy, standing in dark silence beside him, looked up. A light switched on in his head. He, looking first at his father, then over at Paul, said, "No, no, Daddy. We met the naughty lady. You know ... the bad, naughty lady we helped."

Jimmy was trying to add something to the

conversation that he felt had been left out. He knew he remembered. He had a big smile. He knew he remembered.

There was a loud "*whack*" as Mr. Wallace, open palmed, struck the back of Jimmy's head with a hard blow.

"Shut Up!"

The steam came back with mixed anger. The hand was raised again for a second blow. Trooper Joe grabbed the father's wrist before it could strike, again, to the back of Jimmy's head. Jimmy had his hands up, trying to protect himself from what he thought was coming again. It looked like Jimmy was in a defensive position he had taken many times before. The look on the trooper's face was sufficient enough to convince Mr. Wallace he didn't want to strike the lad, or even attempt to raise his hand in Paul's class, again.

"Go on, Jimmy, say what you have to say. It's alright to talk to us," said Paul. The constable used the same calm, convincing, safe tone of voice. He had maintained it since Mr. Wallace first came in. Jimmy continued speaking. He was happy that he could help, that he was being recognized. He had the feeling that he was being important, proud in the fact that anyone wanted to hear what he had to say. He knew he remembered. He was being a good boy!

"The bad lady yelled at me. She yelled at

Daddy, too. Daddy had my gun. She didn't want us to hunt there. She wanted us to leave. She doesn't like hunters. We didn't like her very much, either. She was naughty, she was a naughty lady not to let us hunt there. She was by the house. Daddy yelled at the lady. They were both yelling real loud. She was naughty. Daddy fired my gun. The bad lady fell down in the snow. That's when we went over to her. Don't you remember, Daddy?"

Paul asked him to continue.

"My daddy gave me back my rifle. We went over to the lady in the snow. Don't you remember, Daddy? She was sleeping. She was sleeping in the snow. My daddy picked her up. Right out of the snow he picked her up. My daddy is strong! He picked her up, and he took her into her big house. We put her on the chair, in her kitchen, at the kitchen table. It was a pretty table. I liked the pretty table."

Jimmy paused for a moment. Jimmy had hunted squirrels and chipmunks, had shot a lot of them. Jimmy was a hunter! Shooting a person, however, never entered Jimmy's mind. He then continued.

"There was a flowered tablecloth, with a blue candle in a holder. There were some pretty flowers, in a tall glass, right there, too. Very pretty flowers. I like flowers. I like to smell 'em," he said.

"You remember the pretty flowers, Daddy? ... She was cold ... The lady's hands were very, very cold ... She was still sleeping. I put the pretty blanket on her. The blanket with the deer, with all those pretty birdies on it, to keep her warm. Daddy turned on the stove to keep her warm, too. Don't you remember, Daddy? Daddy didn't like her. She wouldn't let us hunt. She was a naughty lady."

At that point, Jimmy had finished his dissertation.

Mr. Wallace didn't say a thing. Now, his head was looking at the floor. His face had all the color drained out of it. His eyes were quickly twitching back then forth, like a pendulum on a clock. He was a caged animal, looking for any escape route from his immediate surroundings. There was no escape to be found in the small closed room.

"Humph," said Paul, hand on chin.

"Interesting story, don't you think. What do you make of all that?" Paul queried, looking toward the officer at the door. Trooper Joe looked back at Paul, then looked at Mr. Wallace. Mr. Wallace did not look very good. He was cowering in his chair.

"I'm sure we can find some room for him, up at the barracks. We might just have a few more questions we'd like to be answered, there, by Mr. Wallace, here. That is, if he doesn't mind saying a few words." The trooper was giving Mr. Wallace the official state police stare-down.

Mr. Wallace turned into Jell-O, sitting in his chair. He looked like he wanted to say something, do something, move. He wanted to be someplace else but his limbs didn't work, his voice was gone, he had misplaced his thinking cap. He was in a total daze.

Trooper Joseph placed Mr. Wallace in handcuffs. Jimmy, looking on, was confused. Jimmy didn't quite understand what was going on. Why would the nice policeman be going to take his father away someplace? Why does Daddy have handcuffs on? Jimmy looked like he had done something wrong. Paul noticed, went over to him.

"Don't worry, Jimmy. Everything is going to be alright," Paul said, kept repeating it to him. *No! No! Something is wrong! Everything was not all right*, as seen through Jimmy's eyes. Jimmy knew something very bad was happening, very bad, that he didn't understand.

Jimmy just knew something wasn't right. Why were they putting handcuffs on his father? Where were they taking him? His daddy was being directed to the door of Paul's office by the other big man. Jimmy knew the other man was a policeman. He's going with Daddy down the short carpeted hallway, going out the front town hall door. Why did he put Daddy into the police car? Jimmy watched it all. It was taking place in front of him.

"Glad you could stop by, Officer." Paul was lighting his pipe out in front of the town hall.

"Pleasure doing business with you, Sir!" Paul said, taking two good puffs.

In his mind, three or four more pieces of puzzle, jiggling to the left, turned a little to the right, fit nicely into place. Jimmy had tears running down his face. No one had bothered to answer all his questions. Arrangements were made to take the young lad home a half hour later.

The state police cruiser backed out, turned, drove away slowly. The family vehicle which had been parked out front had been left unlocked by Mr. Wallace. It was in the last space on the right. They towed the Wallace vehicle to the state police impound yard. It was as good a place as any to put the car. Details could be worked out to tow the vehicle to the Wallace home, or elsewhere, at a later date.

It was a few weeks later that the entire world found out the news. A trial date came up quickly over at the Newfane Court House. It didn't take very long for the jury to debate, come up with an answer. It came as "*Guilty of Manslaughter*." Mr. Elmer Sherwin Wallace confessed to killing Suzanne Lapan. He confessed to leaving the farmhouse in a condition to easily catch fire, helped it to ignite, to burn as it did. He had hoped the body would never be found, or, if found, everyone would think it was an unfortunate circumstance. No foul play to be suspected at all.

Mr. Wallace had a short fuse when it came to someone yelling at him or his son. He found out loudly, quickly that Suzanne didn't agree with him on hunting rights. That as well as many other this or that's, making his pot boil over that day. He found out he wasn't accustomed to being up against a lady that could raise her voice just as loud as he could. He didn't like that one little bit! His temper took control. Mr. Wallace said he raised the .22, fired without really thinking.

The confessions made the trial short, bittersweet, with no time lost. The jury worked quickly, coming to a verdict in less than a week. They were then excused. Mr. Wallace was sentenced to spend some time in prison. The case was closed.

Whole business came out in every Daily Blab—front page, most of the time. Our local had a picture, head-shoulder shot, of Suzanne Lapan, taken at Rockwell Fleetwood Academy her freshman year. A blown-up, colored picture of the burned remains of the farmhouse. A black-white photo of the house would have told the story just as well. Could have called that picture "*Snow, with black sticks, bent pipes*"! Story to be continued on page seven, column two, beside the comics of the day. Sad tale, really: Jimmy still had no clear idea of why his father had been taken from him. Why Daddy wasn't home with the family? Jimmy didn't understand it at all.

A story of this great magnitude became big news at the Paleyville Diner. Everyone had to know every little tidbit about everything! Paul, the two of us, avoided going there for breakfast for a while, until all the hubbub settled down. When we finally did meet there almost three weeks after the trial had ended, talk of the big doings still lingered on the grapevine. This was local big news! ... Very important business! ... Had to be properly sifted, stirred, with many opinions given.

Same conversations had to be listened to by everyone twenty times over, before ever thinking of putting this old news to rest. Paul couldn't avoid being hounded by well-meaning throngs of people, near or far, that had questions. Questions that Officer Whipple would know the answer to. After all, they felt he was the authority on all matters of the law at all times—day or night. It was his sworn official duty, as the town sheriff, to divulge everything on the subject at hand. This to be done over, and over, and over again. Many, many more times than necessary, as the case might be.

Jimmy Wallace was at home. He had an older sister, Judith, in her thirties, that now looked after him. She cooked, did the laundry, cleaned up after him. Judith, before this occurred, had her own apartment down in Paleyville. Under the recent circumstances, she was allowed to break her rental-year contract, pack up her gear, move back home. The court helped with all the details, legal paperwork. Jimmy still missed his dad. He had no .22, which he missed, too. The state police had taken it.

CHAPTER 13

The world as we knew it was returning to normalcy. Sap was near the end of its run. Boiling was still going full blast at most sugarhouses. There was still plenty of gathered sap, sitting in half-filled storage, that needed to be heated up a bit, turned into syrup. Mud season was upon us. Snow was still around, but not as much of it. Paul was getting things ready to boil. Wanted to start her up that evening. Paul had his sugarhouse out behind his barn. There was a plowed wide path down to it. Paul's driveway went straight past the cabin, all the way back fifty yards to the barn, turned left passing the barn's front, then went around the far side down to the sugarhouse. A five-minute walk, at best, from the cabin.

Michelangelo was all set for a good boil. I was to be their special invited guest. Paul didn't have a large operation, just made enough syrup to keep himself well supplied until the next spring thaw.

Paul had a very unique sugar shack. It was

one of his father's old outbuildings. In the past, it was used as a chicken coop. It was made up of one fairly good-sized room with a high peaked roof. It had two screened chicken-wire openings on either side of the roof line. They were last used for air circulation for the chickens below. Paul had gutted most of the interior, cleaned out all remaining signs of chicken. He himself hosed it out pretty good. In Paul's mind, he had exact conversion plans. The chicken coop would become a sugarhouse.

He had taken thin sheets of plywood, hinged them at the top sides of the four small vents. The vents being at the very top of the coop. With an elaborate pulley system, some screw-in metal loops, plus a goodly length of clothesline, Paul could open, or completely close, the upper openings. He simply loosened or pulled a single cord. The clothesline split to either side near the top. The line ran looped down the interior roof line, then looped more down the middle of the right wall. It was then fastened to a small cleat. Didn't want to make hard work of it. It was easy to loosen, adjust It let in, or out, as much as needed.

The boiling pan, with stove under, was a one-of-a-kind. Paul conjured it up. Somewhere, Paul had picked up an old, quite long wood stove. Most likely at an auction found a few years back. The boiling pan he bought new. The pan was only three feet wide, about four feet long at best. A few inches wider than the stove.

When first built, Paul had unscrewed the cast-iron top from the stove. The stovetop being just over six feet long. The stove width was twenty-six inches wide. Not as wide as the boiling pan. Paul, starting from the back of the stovetop, started welding metal pieces of his design into place. Perfectly slanted, angled up and out, metal strips were welded into place. Each metal piece was about eight inches wide, with all lengths, and widths, measured perfectly.

The widened top was shelved on the inside a half inch down to fit the boiling pan. Welded to exact measurements on all four sides, the enlarged, rectangular opening fit the boiling pan to a tee. This was all done to a secondhand, large, skinny, cast-iron wood stove. It all worked slick as a button!

The stove's long firebox, with renovations above, was front loading. There was some room left over. Just above the firebox door, there were two small, five-inch circular holes. Both with cast-iron covers. Enough room to hold a small coffeepot. The burner holes were sometimes used for an air vent for the firebox below.

Out the back of the stove was a small smokestack. It went straight out the back of the stove for about a foot, then right-angled straight up. The black metal pipe smoked through a vented hole in the roof. Not very much warmth lost. It was a very original, well-working, very neat setup!

Just outside, there was a three hundred gallon, thick plastic bubble tank. It was set up off the ground, about four feet, on a wooden platform. Paul had built the platform especially for the bubble a few years back. Sap from a single pipeline came down from Paul's fifteen-tree maple grove. It would flow across the open field into the tank. It was a straight shot, slightly downhill, into the tank. From the tank, into the sugarhouse, to boil into syrup. Paul had a few metal buckets out, but not very many. If the tank was half filled, Paul was doing better than expected.

The firebox, with pan, took up most of the space in the small, dirt-floored room. It was off-centered slightly. There was three feet of clearance from the firebox's side to the left-side wall. It was the same for the back wall, too. The front wall that had the outside door was more spacious. It had just over five-feet clearance from the stove's front side to the door. The right-side wall was much more spacious as well.

Halfway down the right-side wall, just past the fastened clothesline, Paul put in a very comfortable old-school bus seat. It was up off the ground a foot, supported by an old board foundation. Paul had it all fastened together. The seat, atop the board foundation, was rock solid. It was very sturdy, quite safe to sit on.

Above the seat was a small glassed-in window. It was roughly blocked into place, foam insulated around the edges. That window was very handy. With nasty weather, a person could look outside, get a feel of what was going on out there. No one had to open the door, get covered in snow, freeze to death.

There were two shelves further down on the right side. An arrangement of cleaned mason jars, different sizes, shapes, rubbers with glass covers, lined up. All jars standing ready for the nectar of the gods to be poured into them. To the back wall, right corner, there were three stacks of tin buckets. These were extras, possibly to be used next spring.

"You know much about makin' this stuff?" Paul asked.

"I've seen it enough times, but no, not really," I answered.

Paul was sitting next to me on the school bus.

"Me neither," he said, fumbling in his heavy wool winter coat. He had grabbed hold of something in there, pulled it out.

"Here."

He handed me an unopened pint bottle of Jack Daniels. He fumbled again, pulled out a second bottle for himself.

"I've got it all figured out. When the Jack is gone, the syrup is done!" he exclaimed.

He smiled, the smoke of his pipe mixing with the rising steam. It all drifted high up out the vents.

It was a still, clear night. Full moon, just a whisk of wind rattling the door every so often. We had been there a little over an hour. I was inside, all nice, snug, warm on my bus seat. I didn't have much Jack left. My speech was getting slurred. I wasn't drunk, but I was darn close!

"Coffee time," said Paul, reaching up on the second shelf, coming away with his small perk coffeepot. He ladled out half boiled syrup-sap into the pot, shook some coffee into the round drip through, inside, on top. He replaced the metal tops, set the pot on the small burners. It was perking away nicely in minutes. Paul produced two mugs from someplace unknown. He poured me a mugful.

"You want cream?" he asked. He opened the main door to a blast of cold air. He went out, was back in a moment with a small container of half-and-half. It had been kept cold in the snow.

The coffee was hot! Even with gloves on, the mug was hard to hold on to without grabbing the small, curved loop handle on the side. Half-and-half was added to cool it down a bit. It helped a little. No sugar was needed. The coffee was smooth as silk without it. Coffee had a strong maple flavor that was out of this world.

That coffee was some good stuff! I had a second cup, straight black.

We had a good late evening of it. Don't know exactly how much Paul poured off. It had to be close to four gallons of light-colored gold. It was getting late—time we called it quits. Boy that was really special coffee! Good syrup as well!

The next day, I rode out to Whippletree Lane, down past the stone wall that had been built there thirty years or more ago. Paul's father built that wall, planted the three apple trees I passed before coming to Paul's driveway. Paul was in his workshop: a converted two-car garage.

A rototiller was up on his bench, getting its tines manicured. Paul had his radio tuned in to country. Over to one side, I could see Paul's long flowerboxes. They had been stored out of winter's harm. They had been moved up from the back wall of the shop. They were the next project on the list of spring projects to be tinkered with. Old soil would be mixed with new fertilizer in each box. Then new flowers would go in, mostly geraniums, with a little greenery around the edges. If Paul saw small bulbs or flower sets that looked interesting, they might go into a flowerbox as well. It all depended on what Paul came upon first when visiting the garden center. Everything was mixed with at least two geraniums per box. Had to have geraniums!

His combinations always worked out well. He did make the mistake of putting four-foot iris bulbs in a box one year. There wasn't much light coming through that window that year. Pretty, though!

"Morning," he said as I walked in.

Mike was asleep next to Paul's small wood stove. Paul continued sharpening away as he talked.

"Saw young Jimmy Wallace, yesterday," he started. "Was walking down the road near his house. Police gave him his rifle back. Boy seemed a little happier about that. First time he was out hunting for a spell, I reckon." He blew a smoke ring, looked down at his work.

He turned another tine upward, started sharpening again.

"Peas will be ready to plant soon. Snow is moving out fast. Might only get a few more inches at best, if we get any more at all. I think we're about done with it." He looked, inspected, turned another tine.

"I've been meaning to ask you, Paul," I started, "why you have that sap bucket nailed up on the telephone pole out front?"

"Oh, that." Paul grinned. "That, my boy, is there for tradition!" He blew some smoke.

"You know Bill, up the main road a piece, don't you? Comes down here every year with a new bucket. He tacks it up there, in the same place every year, on that pole. Tells me he's helping me make some syrup. I tell him it's tacked on a goddamn telephone pole. Tell him you won't get sap from that!"

Paul had finished his sharpening detail. I helped him set the machine back on the cement floor, then Paul continued.

"He tells me, he knows full well it's a telephone pole. Then, giving me a good wink, says a flatlander like me wouldn't know the difference! A telephone pole, or a maple tree—both the same tree to me! He thinks that's the funniest joke ever. Does it every year."

Paul, riding high at sixty-eight years young, has lived in Vermont sixty-seven of his sixty-eight years. His parents were on a three-day trip to Hartford, Connecticut. A little business, mixed with a vacation adventure. Mrs. Whipple was pregnant. She was due to deliver in a few weeks. Her water broke, unexpectedly, second day they were down there. She was taken to a Hartford hospital.

Paul was born a little prematurely—in Connecticut, not Vermont. He could never become a true Green Mountain Vermonter. He wasn't born here! Even if he lived in Vermont a hundred years, it wasn't going to happen! How Bill knew where Paul was born we'll never know. A true Vermonter just knows important facts like that. They dig them up to be used on special occasions!

"Think I'll see if I can take Jimmy to hunting camp with me next season," Paul said.

"Be good for him. Get him a deer rifle to use. I can teach him how to track ... Boy! ... If he bagged a buck it would be the thrill of his entire life! ... He'd be happier than a pig in shit! ... That poor kid's been through a lot. Hunting camp would be good for him. Give him some fresh air ... What do you think?" Paul stopped what he was doing.

He looked around, pushed a few things to one side on his bench: it wasn't there. He looked around the shop, found his tobacco pouch on a corner of a flowerbox where he forgot he left it, refilled his pipe.

"I think it's a great idea! ... Jimmy would love it!" I said. We closed up the shop, walked up to the house for a sandwich, maybe a beer to wash it down with.

CHAPTER 14

It was Sunday, bright sun, not much wind, with a touch of mud. The snow was slowly moving out. It was being replaced by large puddles of water, big blue splotches of mush, little riverlets meandering into little streams, further meandering into little ponds of runoff.

The bees were busy at the firehouse. There had been a party for a fireman's young daughter Friday evening. Some of the cleanup was done. There was a lot of cleanup still to do. Mopping of floors, washing down tables, cleaning windows, scrubbing pots, pans in the kitchen. All was on the day's list. Both bathrooms were being made spotless. There was always a good list to keep a soul busy for a morning, or longer.

Other volunteer members were working in the bays. Minor fixes on trucks, checking supplies, brushing dirt, debris off the floors. All dirt on floors was swept out a bay door, then brushed to the side. Cleaned hoses needed rolling. Dirty hoses were being washed. Four bodies were adding, packing tightly, one more length of hose onto an engine. Others were hanging wet hose fresh out of the washer. It was the usual Sunday morning routine, with everyone busy at something. There was always, always something to do.

Someone had bought fresh, homemade peanut butter cookies. Two family-size pizza boxes were quickly losing pieces from within. Someone else brought brownies. Coffee was on, being consumed. A little more than half a pot was left on a burner. The doughnuts were fresh, plentiful. These men, or women, worked hard keeping everything in tip-top condition. They deserved to eat well, too.

A cruiser with a whip antenna came down Fireman's Trail slowly. It pulled to one side, toward the open door of bay two. It then backed across Fireman's to park in a puddle. Smoke was drifting out the driver-side window. You could see the silhouette of a large dog's head in the back seat. Paul, Mike in back, had arrived to see what the Bee-Buzz was for the day.

Paul looked down, shut off his engine with a twist of the car key ... *Ping!* ... *Crack!* ... Something hit the center of his windshield. The front glass of Paul's vehicle shattered into a thousand tiny pieces. Small shards, pieces of safety glass, filled the entire front seat. Paul was totally showered. His lap was full of glittering glass diamonds. Outside, on the front of his vehicle, more shards had rained down, covering the cruiser's hood, then falling off both sides into the wet snow, mud, rippled puddles.

"What the hell ... ?" Paul said, mostly to himself. It had startled him. Mike had taken notice from the back seat. Paul crouched down, took his left hand, hooked the door opener. His right hand was on the top of his revolver holster. Very cautiously, he started opening the cruiser door.

"Stay down, Mike! Down, boy! Down!" Mike lowered himself down, low, across in the back seat. He knew what "down" meant. He was well trained.

Another "*Ping*" hit the driver-side door, low, ricocheted off. The small-caliber bullet left a good dent, removing the paint, showed metal. It didn't have the power to go through the entire door. It did have the power to penetrate human flesh, however!

Paul took a quick look forward. He saw nothing unusual or out of place. He looked again. His second peek revealed what he was looking for. Something, or someone, moved. It caught his attention quickly. Something moved by the corner of the building. It was a person. A person, crouched behind a fifty-gallon oil barrel. A small figure.

Paul wasn't sure who it was at first. He couldn't quite catch the face to perceive who it was clearly. The figure moved a few feet. Now, Paul was very sure what he was looking at!

Jimmy Wallace? ... It was Jimmy Wallace! ... His .22 was pointed in Paul's direction. He was now hunkered down behind the fifty-gallon drum.

"Jimmy! ... What the hell are you doing?" Paul yelled out at him. Curious heads turned in the bays. The hoses stopped being rolled. They, too, wondered what was happening. No one moved.

"You're Bad! ... You're a naughty man! ... You took my daddy! ... I want my daddy! You're naughty!" Jimmy screamed back at him, his voice in tears. He ducked down behind the oil drum even further.

"You put that gun down right now! ... Right now, Jimmy! ... Put it down!" Paul commanded in a loud authoritarian voice. Paul took another peek. Jimmy hadn't moved. "NOW, JIMMY!"

Jimmy was scared. He didn't know exactly what he should do, or not do. His mind hadn't gotten there yet. He started to raise the rifle. "Don't point it! ... Put it on the ground, Jimmy ... NOW!" Jimmy just stood motionless. He looked right at Paul, then looked down. He tossed the gun into the wet snow beside him. Jimmy was still standing, three-quarters concealed behind the big barrel, not sure what to do next. He wanted to be someplace else, he knew that. He didn't want to be there anymore.

Young Mr. Wallace abrupty turned around. He ran down the outside of the building, toward the openness of a cornfield a distance before him. The field was snow covered, deep pud-dled, covered in deep mud. He took a last look, changed his course. Jimmy disappeared around the back corner of the firehouse.

Caleb, J.J. on a garden hose, was cleaning the hot-dog/hamburger grill out behind. The grill had been used heavily. The birthday par-ty made a lot of grease. It was full of splatter, needing cleaning badly. Caleb heard, then saw, someone coming fast.

"Jimmy? ... What the—," Caleb said, looking up, seeing it was Jimmy for the first time.

"Outtah my way! ... Outtah my way! ... Outtah my way!" Jimmy yelled, running past them with his arms flailing. Jimmy saw the back door to the fire station was held open by a pipe pole. The pole was propped tightly to the door handle on one end. The other end was stuck in the snow. Jimmy ran through the opening. He was now inside.

He found himself confronting several new members of the department he had never seen before. All frozen in their places, staring at him. All wondering what was going on. Jimmy froze momentarily as well. He then ran toward the only open door he saw. George was just inside the doorway Jimmy was looking at.

George will move! I'll make him move! I can get by him. I'll be back outside. Jimmy's mind was racing just as fast as his feet were moving. Jimmy soon found out he had made a mistake. Looking past George, he discovered hoses hanging down with many ropes hitched to the walls. The small room had no exit. He was looking past the door to the interior of the hose tower. He had run right into a cul-de-sac.

George was just inside the hose tower. He had on his turn-out gear. Coat-pants-boots-helmet-gloves, well protected. You could see the sweat pouring off his face from hauling lines. He had been working the wet lines up to the tower top. He saw Jimmy, he stepped back.

Jimmy stood in the doorway, encircled by firemen wondering what was going on. He reached into the front pocket of his pullover yellow jacket. He produced a black-handled, serrated-edged steak knife. The blade of it was bent slightly, in a slow curve. It was long enough, pointed, sharp enough to do some damage. Jimmy started swinging it back, then forth in front of him. It then was waved over his head, wildly flailing his arms about in the air. He looked at George, then at the audience, then quickly back at George.

"Stay away, stay away, stay away, stay away! ... You're all bad people! ... Naughty, naughty bad people! ... Stay away or I'll cut him, I'll cut him! ... Stay away!" Jimmy, surrounded, stepped into the hose tower. He was swinging the knife madly in George's direction. George stepped back again. He was backed up against the wall. Only, many lines attached to cleats behind him. Both Jimmy, George in front of him, were surrounded by hanging hose lines. All in various stages of drying out.

Jimmy swung his bent steak knife in George's direction, then swung it over his head again. George was against the wall. He could feel two cleats digging through the back of his heavy coat. His gloved hands opened quickly, letting a taut line go free. The whirring of a rope line, swiftly going through a pulley, could be heard distinctly.

Young Wallace had just enough time to look up, try to shield himself, before the mass of inch-and-a-half line came crashing down. The "s" hook caught Jimmy right above his left eye, causing a bad laceration. Jimmy's knees buckled. He had both arms raised up. The hose kept coming down—fast, hard. Jimmy fell, his hands, body, pushed down by the weight coming at him. He was quickly buried under hose on the cement floor. One foot was sticking out the door. No movement. George was up to his knees in hose, but otherwise not hurt.

It only took a moment before the tower was full of firemen pulling at the hose. There was blood—a lot of blood. It was on the hose, on the cement floor, on Jimmy. It was J.J. that realized where the blood was all coming from. Jimmy was cut. He was cut badly.

When the hose came down, Jimmy's hands went up. It was a defensive move in desperation on Jimmy's part. He was trying to protect himself. The weight of the hose quickly took control. It brought the hand holding the steak knife down sharply. The serrated blade cut deeply into the side of Jimmy's neck. The hose line kept falling, leaving behind a jagged three-inch laceration where a deep laceration should not be. A nasty, spurting wound caused by a serrated blade across the throat. The blood was gushing, bubbling, uncontrolled.

Everything that could be done medically was started. Trauma dressings were applied, then more dressings added over the first. Jimmy looked up with a blank dark stare. He didn't say anything. There was blood at the corner of his mouth. His eyes slowly started closing.

Greg had run to dispatch.

"KAY 445, this is WIL 846 calling ... Priority! ... Priority!" Luckily, Kayle wasn't busy. They came right on.

"WIL 846."

Greg keyed the microphone.

"Please dispatch an ambulance to our station, ASAP. We have an approximately thirteen-year-old male, with bad lacerations to his face and neck. Bleeding is not fully controlled. He's still losing blood. Incident happened about three minutes ago. EMTs are here on the scene. We need a paramedic here bad ... Come code 3!" Greg was winded, but he got it all out.

"We copy, WIL 846," Kayle answered.

Within a half minute, Kayle Central had Blue Angel's A-2 ambulance responding. Blue Angel responded with a second ambulance, two more medical technician intermediates on board moments later. Blue Angel's paramedic was on the scene of another, different medical call. She heard what was going on, could free herself up, would respond directly to the scene at our station. Her ETA would be three minutes away.

Paul, of course, was there. Trooper Joe, driving in just to visit, had no idea of the situation. He responded quickly, tried to lend a helping hand wherever he could. A lot of people were on standby, wanting to help, trying to stay out of the way.

There was a small swarm, all trying in vain to bring Jimmy back to life. CPR was started when they no longer could feel any pulse. Breathing slowed, then stopped. Gloved hands were counting: ten, eleven, twelve. A BVM, bag-valve mask, used to give oxygen and help a person breathe, was being squeezed on cue with high-flow oxygen attached. There was no more blood seeping through the well-dressed wound. The paramedic was on the scene.

Twelve minutes had gone by since the hose dropped. Every emergency medical practice we had available was used. Every "should have," "would have," and "could have" was played out, done quickly, professionally.

We went by the book, did everything right, perfect even, to the letter. Only trouble was, it was all done too late. All done in vain! It wasn't supposed to end the way it did! We did everything we could! Young Jimmy Wallace died that day—in our hose tower, in our fire station. Sometimes, things just don't work out the way the world, or our little community, would like them to.

We were at the diner the next Friday. It was a songbird-singing day. The temp had risen into the lower sixties. The sun was out. It had warmed up quite a bit. It was actually nice outside. A few folk even had short sleeves on, with shorts.

Everyone at the diner wanted Paul's undivided attention. They had to talk about the past events that happened at the Westland Fire Station. The scuttle moves very quickly. If the papers hadn't had the news on the front pages yet, word of mouth traveled just as fast. Paul was not interested in discussing any part of the recent mess. The strongly insistent ones that kept insisting on answers had smoke blown in their face. After saying no to them three times or more, they deserved more than just smoke! Paul's smoke did all the talking for him. There was very little worth saying.

"An instrument for measuring the specific gravity of liquids ... ten letters ..." In four-part harmony, full bodied, with a lot of gusto, came the rousing, one-word chorus ...

"Hydrometer!"

At least ten people said it together. It was great! Betty almost popped off her seat! She looked around at all the knowing faces, then wrote the answer down. Seems there were a few sap gatherers gathered in attendance today! The Sapsucker Chorus was all tuned up, having a good breakfast away from the wood pile, and sap boiling, that morning!

"...For Westland, smoke investigation looking south from the village. No other information available at this time. 1613, Dispatcher Four."

CPSIA information can be obtained
at www.ICGtesting.com
Printed in the USA
FSHW010330190221
78716FS